CW01651282

PISTOLS AT DAWN

AND OTHER SHORT STORIES

By Dick Hamilton

COVER PHOTO

This picture shows Dick Hamilton taking his M.A. in Screenwriting degree at Liverpool John Moores University in about 2000 A.D.

He already had an M.A. in Law from Oxford University. He was a Liverpool barrister for 30 years, during which he wrote a History of the Northern Circuit (FOUL BILLS AND DAGGER MONEY) and also a History of the Bar (ALL JANGLE AND RIOT). He was also for three years the Film Critic of the Liverpool Daily Post. Then he was a Circuit judge for 11 years.

This book is published in 2019 by Sue Newton Publishing, The Court House, 24 South Road, Grassendale Park, Liverpool L19 OLT.

Printed by Rayross Print Factory Limited, Liverpool.

Dick Hamilton has asserted his moral right to be identified as the author of this work in accordance with the Copyright, Design and Patents Act 1988.

ISBN -10-9544819-3-3
ISBN- 13-978-0-9544819-3-3 **Price £10.00**

INTRO

I love reading short stories. My all-time favourites are Jack London's *To Build a Fire*, in its second version, and Henry Lawson's *The Drover's Wife,* an Australian story. Of course I love other well-known stories, such as O. Henry's *The Gifts of the Magi*, Guy de Maupassant's *The Necklace*, and P.G. Wodehouse's *The Great Sermon Handicap*.

But I love writing short stories too. Here, then, is a selection of 25 of mine under the title *Pistols at Dawn*. They are all original and include ghost stories, love stories, murder stories, comedies and dramas. They come from my imagination, and have no relation to existing persons.

Dick Hamilton

Liverpool, 7th June 2019

CONTENTS

PISTOLS AT DAWN

Paris in 1905. Lt. Gaston Fourchet, of the Fifth Hussars, was so used to being admired by young officers who joined the regiment, that he could not believe it when one of them accused him of cheating at cards.

'My dear fellow,' he would say to a youngster whom he had fleeced, 'Better luck next time, eh?'

Yet a new officer, Lt. Rene Lenoir, accused him of cheating. Gaston turned to the others.

'Am I not to be trusted?' he said, embracing them all with his winning smile.

'Of course,' they all said.

But Rene stood his ground. 'Hand me that pack of cards, he said, and held them up one by one, with their backs to him.

'The three of clubs,' he said of the topmost card, and threw it face upwards onto the table. Sure enough, it was the three of clubs.

'King of Diamonds,' he said, in the same way. So it was.

'Ace of Hearts,' he said next, and so it turned out to be.

'Given a tinted pair of glasses like yours,' Rene said, 'I can read every single card from behind.'

They were both wearing slightly tinted glasses, and Rene flung the rest of the cards in Gaston's face.

Gaston had only one course open to him.

'I demand satisfaction,' he said. 'Pistols at dawn tomorrow morning?'

'Yes,' said Rene, 'the Avengers.'

The Avengers were a pair of pistols which were displayed in the Officers' Mess. They had often been used in past regimental duels. They were manufactured identically so that neither gave the other an advantage. They had extra long barrels, to ensure maximum accuracy, though at a distance of 20 paces the utmost accuracy is not needed. Rene Lenoir was said to be an excellent shot. Gaston had fought many duels himself. Here he was now, with perhaps only a few hours to live. A single shot might blind him in one eye, or hit him in the stomach, a slow and agonizing death.

All the formalities were arranged. The duel was to be fought in the cobbled courtyard of the regimental stables – the Bois de Boulogne was far too public, even at dawn. A shot inside the barracks would bring no strangers in.

Gaston had fought too many duels to bother about one more. It would be as well to kill his opponent outright. He turned up several minutes before the appointed hour, smiling nonchalantly. Bah! It would be all over in a minute. The seconds loaded the pistols with fastidious care, and Gaston let Rene choose his weapon. The Major who was supervising the proceedings announced the rules carefully, though Gaston knew them all by heart. Then he withdrew, and left the two men standing back to back. Each was to take ten paces, counted aloud, and then turn and fire. Both duellists nodded agreement.

The counting started.

'One!' Gaston merely smiled, and took his pace forward. Should he let Rene live? He thought not.

'Two!' Gaston wondered how he would spend that evening. Wine and women, preferably. He did not care for singing.

'Three!' Lots of people fought several duels, he knew. Pushkin, the young Russian poet, had fought 28 duels . But there was one more, he remembered, in which Pushkin was fatally wounded.

'FOUR!' He was making his paces more heavily now, and the sweat started from his brow. Nobody's luck lasts forever, and perhaps his was running out now.

'FIVE!' Rene was too keen to fight a duel, and had chosen "the Avengers" as weapons. In the last duel which had been fought with them, both duellists received fatal injuries.

'SIX!' If Gaston's boots had been made of lead, it could not have been more difficult to take another pace forward. Instant death would not be so bad, but suppose it was a death of long slow agony? Or suppose a disabling injury left him a cripple for life?

'SEVEN!' In three more paces it would be too late to withdraw. He could throw down his pistol, or fire it in the air. And the whole regiment would know that he had funked it. He would be branded forever as a coward.

'EIGHT!' He could not move his legs.

'Take your next step now!' the Major ordered. He managed to do so, but the seconds exchanged glances.

'NINE' Only one more pace, and Rene would surely win.

He would look so smug. Gaston had no alternative. He wheeled round and fired at Rene's back. Rene shrugged his shoulders, dropped his pistol, sank to his knees, and sprawled full-length on the ground. Dead. His seconds rushed to the body, but the Major walked straight across to Gaston. He seized Gaston's pistol, and tossed it to his seconds.

'I thought you shouted 'Ten', Gaston said feebly to him.

The Major struck him hard in the face with the back of his hand. The seconds on both sides put their heads together. Gaston deserved to die, but they were not entitled to shoot him.

'You are under arrest,' the Major said, and sent him at once to his Commanding Officer.

Col. Aristide Dieudonné had already heard all the circumstances before Gaston came before him. But what was he to do? If word got out, it would mean disgrace for the whole regiment, perhaps the whole Army as well. The Army was already in disgrace from the Dreyfus affair, where they had conspired to frame Lt. Dreyfus on the charge of spying. Gaston could not possibly go unpunished.

Stripping him of his rank was not enough, and imprisonment would seem too tame. But he thought quickly, and reached a decision.

'What have you to say to me, Lt. Fourchet?' He said.

'I miscounted the paces, tragically, and fired too soon,' said Gaston. He was wasting his words.

'You have been a Lieutenant,' said the Colonel dryly, 'for seven years now. Too long.'

Gaston assumed he was going to be stripped of his rank, but he was wrong.

'It is time that you were promoted,' said the Colonel, 'to the rank of Captain. As from today.'

Gaston could have shouted for joy.

'And you will be posted immediately to a command of great responsibility. The prison station of Devil's Island, for the period of ten years. Ten years continuously, with no leave allowed. Have you any questions?'

Gaston was too flabbergasted to speak. For ten years he would be in command of prisoners. But his duties would confine him to Devil's Island, with no relief. No interests, or pleasures.

'You may go,' said the Colonel.

Gaston saluted, and left the room. He was still alive, that was the main thing. Lt. Dreyfus had spent 5 years on Devil's Island, and had survived. But could he himself survive for that long? Devil's Island was known as "the Dry Guillotine," because prisoners died without shedding blood. Their bodies were thrown to the crocodiles, which saved having funeral services.

It was almost too good to be true. He still had his life and liberty. Ten years was a long time, but it would pass. He would make it pass, from a strict application to his duties, leaving no time for remorse. His official reports and his attention to duty met with the approval of his seniors. The prisoners were given all the attention they deserved, and the food they were entitled to. No more nor less. He was a model prison governor, and when the ten years were up, he returned to France a changed man. He had aged considerably. He walked with a stoop, and had a hacking cough. His face was much sunken, but he could still walk with pride. Indeed, on his return to Paris, he was given a medal for

Distinguished Service, being the only Governor of Devil's Island to receive that honour. He retired from the service on half pay, as was usual, and lived quietly in a cheap little hotel in Paris where nobody bothered him. Occasionally he looked at his medal with a wistful smile. It was so much less than he had hoped for when a dashing young officer. One night, on the anniversary of the famous duel, he was returning to his hotel when somebody stepped out of the shadows and stopped him with a hand to his chest

'Let me pass, sir,' said Gaston.

'No,' said the young man, a Lieutenant in the 5th Hussars.

''What do you want?' said Gaston.

'You,' said the Lieutenant, 'or rather, your life.'

'I've got no money, if that's what you want,' said Gaston.

'Let me introduce myself,' said the Lieutenant. 'My name is Henri Lenoir, the son of the man you murdered so long ago.'

'That was many years ago,' said Gaston.

'But this isn't,' said Henri striking him across the face with a pair of gloves. 'I demand satisfaction. You are going to fight a duel with me. A fair one.'

. 'All right,' said Gaston hopelessly. 'When?'

'Tomorrow dawn,' said Henri. 'In the same place. There are many fellow-officers who would be glad to act as your seconds.'

'So be it,' said Gaston.

Accordingly at dawn the two antagonists found themselves face to face in the stable yard. Major Bompierre was there to supervise proceedings, and the rules were the same.

'ONE!' said the Major, and they each took a pace away from each other.

'TWO!' said the Major, and the same thing happened. But when he came to NINE!, he was appalled to see Gaston turn and face his opponent, who had his back to him. He raised his pistol in the air.

Surely, the Major thought in horror, he is not going to play the same trick again. But this time Gaston fired his pistol uselessly into the air, and then dropped it.

'TEN!' said the Major., and Henri turned to face Gaston. He had all the time in the world to take careful aim. It would be like shooting a sitting duck. Nevertheless, he had his father's murder to avenge.

Gaston stood there with a slight smile upon his lips, and waited for what seemed an eternity.

A BIT MUCH

The Bishop's study lay in darkness. Golf clubs leant against dim shelves of earnest books. Sporting trophies glinted on either side of a clock on the mantelpiece with a solid, reassuring tick. Near the door there was a faint luminance, as of soft summer moonlight.

Footsteps strode towards the door, which was flung open. The Bishop, a tall figure, stood against the light from the hall.

'Come on out' he said. 'I know you're there'.

The faint luminance was now in the corner by the curtains; when the lights were turned on it became a faint shimmer, like a heat haze. But as the clock began to chime eleven the shimmer brightened, filled out, and became the Rev. Douglas Spoon, deceased.

'I might have known it', said the Bishop. 'What are you doing here at this time of night, Duggie?'

'It's my time of night', said Duggie; 'I always walk now.'

'But Why here?'

'Why do you think?' Said Duggie 'I fell down your stairs ten years ago. You helped carry me in here yourself, Jack.'

'And for the last two weeks you've been coming back, and upsetting my spaniels. I thought this study felt a bit chilly for June.'

'All right, Jack', said Duggie huffily; 'if you don't want me, I'll go.'

He started to walk through the wall.

'Come back this minute!' Said Jack. 'Sit down where I can keep my eye on you; we're having none of your old tricks now.'

'I don't know what you mean,' said Duggie.

'You do', said Jack. 'That's Daphnes' room, and she's gone to bed.'

'You can't think –'

'I CAN think and I DO think. it was bad enough with you and Miss Lightwell in the vestry –'

'We were only –'

'I know what you were only. But if the verger hadn't come in it would have been a good deal furthermore. That's why Daphne broke off the engagement, and not a moment too soon. A fine brother –in-law you'd have made! And then, instead of taking it like a man, you got drunk,and fell down my stairs.'

'Not drunk', said Duggie; 'just a weeny bit stuccoed.'

'Stuccoed?' asked Jack

'It's what we used to say at Tbeological College. It means 'elegantly plastered.'

'I remember', laughed Jack. 'But your trouble was you never learnt to take things seriously after our student days.'

'I most certainly did.'

'I'm afraid you did not. You were too keen on barmaids, for a start.'

'I was not.'

'To say nothing of student nurses'

He spoke to thin air. Duggie had vanished. He materialized a moment later behind Jack's chair, wearing a white sheet.

'BOO!' He shouted.

Jack sighed heavily. After a pause, Duggie materialized again in his chair, looking rather ashamed of himself.

'Even if I did,' he said, 'a chap's entitled to his fun.'

'Not like that as a Vicar, he isn't', said Jack.

'It was years ago, anyway. I've learned my lesson.'

'You were just trying to get into Daphne's room,'

'I'm on the Other Side now,' said Duggie; 'you can't stop me.'

'Don't count on that,' said Jack evenly.

'Look', shouted Duggie in a fury, 'I know I'm only an ex-vicar, and you're the blasted Bishop, but a ghost's got to haunt the place he was last connected with. Didn't they teach you anything at Theologial College?

'Rather more than they taught you chasing barmaids,' said the Bishop. 'Besides –'

He slid open a drawer in a filing cabinet and took out a card. '– You had already been appointed to Stubford Rectory. When you died you were only here on a social call. I think – he replaced the filing card and closed the door quietly –it would be better for all concerned if you returned there straight away. We'll review your position in 6 months' time. I fancy –' he smiled quietly – 'you will then be in a more chastened frame of mind.'

'Who's the new Rector there?' asked Duggie.

'Canon Crammer,' said Jack, ominously.

Duggie turned slightly opaque, like a window in frost.

'Does he still', he said hollowly, 'go for early morning sprints in his tight running shorts?'

'So I understand', said Jack. 'And then, after a cold shower,' he practices his sermons. Aloud. Now be off with you. We'll leave it like that for 6 months.'

'So I've got to stay there for six months?'

'Yes,' said Jack.

With Canon Crammer?'

'Yes,' said Jack.

'Does he still tell that story about the Archdeacon's golfing umbrella?'

'Interminably,' said Jack.

'Well,' said Duggie, starting to disappear, so that his last words hung on the empty air, 'I do think that's a bit much!'

ALL CLEAR

Nellie Minto sat at the kitchen table at 9 Stockton Street, her little terrace house, looking thoughtfully at the beautiful sunset. Soon it would be time to put on the lights and draw the blackout curtains. She needed no reminder to do it; Stockton Street was too near the docks for comfort, where the enemy bombs fell night after night. The clear nights were always the worst.

She looked at her ration books. There were two little squares left in for the week's meat rations, which the butcher would cut out in return for a very modest joint, or four chops. Ken was due home on leave, and she'd like to have something welcoming for him. He got fed well enough in the Army, to be sure, but it wasn't the same as a good home-cooked meal. He always said how he missed her apple dumplings; there was more than one meaning you could put on that.

His letters home were not very detailed; they were not allowed to be, for censorship reasons. Ken had been posted to a searchlight unit on the east coast, where they watched for Jerry planes crossing the North Sea on their nightly raids. Of course there were some risks - a Jerry bomber might unload its bombs onto their searchlight post, or try to machine-gun their probing searchlights into splinters of metal and glass. But they suffered far fewer casualties than the infantry. Nellie had seen too many infantry wives standing on their doorsteps reading the official telegrams.

‘We regret to inform you…’ they always started.

Quite often, Ken’s unit brought down a German plane.

‘We had a great sunset last night,’ he’d written, and she knew what he meant. Once he even wrote ‘We had five great sunsets this week.’

How proud she was of him! For him the Air Raid siren was a call to action; for her, it meant desperate nights, wondering whether she’d wake up in a house all ruined, or even wake up at all.

In Stockton Street the siren went whoo-hoo-hoo, with the whooping, looping sound of the Alert. It was so different from the All Clear signal, a long whooo, with the single unbroken high note, like the song of angels.

Nellie sighed heavily, and put the ration books away carefully in the kitchen drawer. They would be quite safe unless the whole house was reduced to rubble. Who’d be alive to need them then? She thought.

There was usually a quarter of an hour between the Alert and the start of the bombing. Her daughter Shirley was sitting at the same kitchen table; she had been doing her homework ever since Children’s Hour finished on the wireless. She looked up steadily with her serious grey eyes as her mother came in, and nodded obediently. She gathered up her things, and took them with her to the foot of the stairs. She sat there reading her lesson. It only took a moment to duck under the stairs and shut the cupboard door, should the bombs come.

There was a distant rumble of approaching planes. Nellie looked out into the garden. Walter, their black cat, was sitting under a tree. Little Tommy was completely absorbed in making a plasticine model of him.

'In, Tommy, quick!' shouted Nellie.

'Nearly finished, Mum,' he said. 'I'll just get Walter. Can't leave him outside.'

He grabbed at Walter, which was a mistake. Walter gave an indignant miaow, and skittered over the garden wall.

Tommy went racing after him through the back door into the alley, but his mother seized him by the collar, and started to haul him into the house.

'I said Come inside and I meant Come inside,' said Nellie. 'You don't want Adolf Hitler to get you.'

'Or Walter!' Said Tommy. 'I won't let him get Walter.'

He wriggled round in his mother's grasp, and bit her hard on the hand. She swore, and let go. Tommy was out of the back gate in a flash, running down the alley towards the main road.

The deep red sky faded into blackness. The rumbling of planes grew .louder. With all the curtains drawn in the street, it was pitch dark. On the horizon, searchlights fingered the sky, criss-crossing their beams, and searching for enemy planes. Every now and then they caught one, and held onto it as long as they could, while the Ack-ack guns tried to bring it down. Ken would be doing that too, thought Nellie. But, down by the docks, there were so many planes, and so few beams. The angry crump! crump! of exploding bombs came again and again. A burst of orange light showed that a petrol tanker had been hit.

Tommy was headed that way.

Nellie pounded after him as fast as she could, reached the end of the alley, and turned into the main road. An Air Raid Warden ran towards her.

‘Get back indoors!’ he commanded, seeking to block her path. She dodged round him, and had left him far behind when an urgent voice hissed to her, ‘Hey, missus, is he yours?”

An elderly man, standing on the front doorstep of his house, had hold of Tommy.

‘I want Walter!’ wailed Tommy, as she picked him up in her arms and ran back to her house.

‘He’ll be all right,’ lied Nellie, ‘he’s gone to visit some cat friends who live in a cellar round here.’

‘Promise?’ whimpered Tommy.

‘I promise’ said his mother, ‘and as a special treat, on Saturday I’ll take you and Shirley to see the Tarzan film. It’s on at the Roxy.’

Soon, Shirley and Tommy were nestled under the stairs – it was snug and comforting to them - and Nellie curled up under the kitchen table. Nothing short of a direct hit could harm them - the windows were criss-crossed with sticky tape, to reduce the risk of glass splinters, if the curtains had not been drawn. The front and back doors were locked and bolted, and the Jerries could do their worst.

The Jerries did their worst. On Commercial Road the Roxy cinema was reduced to ashes by an incendiary bomb, before the end of the Gary Cooper film; forty people lost their lives. The Rose and Crown pub had been flattened too; the landlord was lucky to be still alive, but he had shut up and gone down to the cellar the moment that the bombs began to fall. The rescue teams were busy all night digging families out of the rubble down by the docks, and it was a miracle that the gasworks had not gone up in smoke. But Nellie and her family escaped unharmed, and even before dawn the enemy planes had gone. The siren sounded the

All Clear, and life began again.

Nellie got up quietly and made a pot of tea. The children were still fast asleep under the stairs, God bless 'em. She drew back the curtains and peeped out; fires were still burning down by the docks, and her nostrils caught the sharp smell of smoke. The sky turned gold, to celebrate the new day. The milkman made his delivery, and the paper-boy came. Nellie went to wake the children, and hugged them as they yawned and stretched.

'You've been so good,' she said, 'there'll be scrambled eggs for breakfast.'

She made big helpings for the children, and scraped out the last of the tin of dried eggs for herself. Shirley wanted her mother to have more of her share, but she refused.

'You're growing up,' she said. 'Your Dad would be so proud of you!'

All of a sudden there was a meow from outside the back door. Walter arrived, looking a little worse for wear. His fur was all wet from water from the fire hoses, and he smelt strongly of smoke.

'You're not coming in here all sooty!', said Nellie severely, wiping him down with a rough towel before she let the children cuddle him.

She switched on the eight-o-clock news, which spoke of wide-spread raids, and many German planes shot down. There were heartening words of heroism from Winston Churchill, and then some dance-band music. The children put on their coats and satchels, and left hand-in-hand for school; it was not far.

Nellie, in her apron and headscarf, took a bucket and soap and went to scrub the front door-step. It was a matter of pride to her that it was always snow-white, no matter what. She waved to Mrs. Finnegan across the road.

'Still in one piece, eh!' she called cheerily.

'All's well with us,' called Mrs. Finnegan.

She saw the postman coming down the road, and her heart rose up. Thursdays usually bought a letter from Ken.

With a cheery smile the postman delivered the post to No. 3, and No. 5, and No. 7. But before he left No. 7, he straightened the sack on his back, and checked carefully to make sure he had the right delivery for No. 9.

Nellie's heart plummeted. She had seen it happen all too often in Stockton Street. He had only one envelope to hand to her, a small brown envelope in official style.

'I hope it's not bad news, Mrs. Minto,' he said.

'I hope so too,' she replied, and took it from him.

She opened it steadily, then read and re-read its short, simple message.

'We regret to inform you –' it said.

She turned away from the postman dry-eyed, but her lips trembled.

'I'm going to be brave,' she said firmly to herself. 'I'm going to be very, very brave.'

She went back into the house and closed the door quietly behind her.

ALL MOD. CONS.

After the sun had set, the famous gardens of Hawkesley Manor were fragrant with summer perfume, and the lights of the Manor went out one by one.

Inside the Great Hall, moonlight picked out swords and shields on the walls, and the suit of armour at the head of the great staircase. As a grandfather clock chimed midnight, a transparent leg stepped cautiously out of the wall in the upstairs passage. The rest of a bearded middle-aged man emerged, in Elizabethan costume, with a sword. No-one else was in sight. It was safe for him to appear fully..

As the ghost approached the Long Gallery his hand brushed accidentally against a little brass plate in the wall, and the Gallery was suddenly flooded with electric light. He sprang back in terror, his transparency ebbing and flowing like a beating heart. When he calmed down, he continued to a line of portraits, and nodded a greeting first to a Crusader.

Further along the row he bowed before the portrait of his father, a kindly-looking man. Then he came to his own picture. A plaque beneath it said "Sir Edward Hawkesley, 1548-1602.

He looked at himself as if in a mirror, and straightened his ruff and hat.

Almost at the end of the line was the eighteenth Earl of

Hawkesley, in yachting-cap and flannels, nonchalantly smoking a cigarette, and leaning against an open-topped sports car. Sir Edward had never seen him before, and was so intrigued by everything in the picture, that he failed to notice the final portrait. Sir Hugo, the present Earl, had been painted in the modern Francis Bacon squidgy style, which made it grotesque. Sir Edward suddenly saw it. He gave a shriek of terror, backed hastily away against the suit of armour, clutched at it for support, and toppled headlong with it down the stairs. There was a fearful series of clatters and crashes, and he sat stunned at the bottom, the casque somehow lodged upon his head.

He staggered to a table in the centre of the hall on which stood an empty glass and a bottle of colourless liquid. He filled the glass, and downed it in one gulp. It was vodka. The ceiling and the floor seemed suddenly to collide.

Somewhere off the Great Hall a door opened, and light spilled into the room. Polly, a charming teenage girl in striped pyjamas, her blonde hair cut in pageboy style, marched in with the fearless courage of the Hawkesley line.

'Who's there?' she said.

Sir Edward, his throat still afire, could only gasp.

'Why', she said, 'it's someone in fancy dress! No, it isn't; surely – it's Sir Edward, isn't it? I know you from your portrait.'

'Do you, young sir?'

'I'm not a sir, I'm a girl!'

'In such accoutrements?' Asked Sir Edward.

'Lots of girls wear pyjamas these days', said Polly, 'What are you doing here?'

'Tis exactly four hundred years since I died. I come here every hundred years.'

'But I can touch you! I thought all ghosts were thin transparent things.'

'With most of my kind, it is so. I have the more substance, from appearing so seldom.'

'I'm Polly. So you're my great-great-great-great – whatever. . Can I call you Grandad?'

'For sure. But may I have a glass of true water? This one comes from the fires of hell.'

'If you want water, there's a tap in the downstairs cloakroom.'

She led him through a door at the side of the room.

'Here's a glass,' she said, handing him one off the shelf.

'And, methinks, an indoor well. I shall fill my glass from it.'

'That's not a well, it's the loo!'

'What, forsooth?'

'The loo. The toilet. The -' she hunted for a word he would know – 'the privy.'

'Like none I ever saw. How does it work, pray?'

'I'll show you.'

She tore some pieces from a pink toilet roll, scrunched them up into balls, and dropped them into the bowl.

'Then I press the handle, down. So.'

The toilet roared into action. Sir Edward watched open-mouthed as the water raced the pink balls round and round, till they suddenly vanished downwards.

'A miracle! Would it also work at my behest?'

'Every time,' said Polly.

So Sir Edward tried it, and tried it again, and again, and again.

'First the flood of light in this house,' he said, 'then the water of fire, then this enchanted whirlpool,' he said. 'Have you any further wonders to show me?'

'Of course. We've got all mod. cons here. How long can you stay, Grandad?'

'Till sunrise. Then I return to the land of shadows.'

'There's so much we could talk about', said Polly wistfully. 'Did you ever meet Queen Elizabeth?'

'Many times, my child.'

'Was she really the Virgin Queen?'

'Virginity,' said Sir Edward stiffly, 'is not a matter for the tongues of gentlefolk.'

'Oh,' said Polly breezily, 'the girls at school talk about virginity all the time. Some of us have still got ours.'

Sir Edward looked profoundly shocked.

'Sorry, Grandad,' said Polly. 'But tell me something else. When the Spanish Armada came, did Sir Francis Drake win the game of bowls?'

'Indeed he did. I lost!' Said Sir Edward indignantly. 'It is my belief that he cheated. While we were looking out to sea, he moved his wood nearer the jack. I would stake my oath upon it.'

'Still, you beat the Spaniards.'

'We did. Now tell me a little about yourself.'

'When I'm 19, I want to sail round the world,' sad Polly.

'Mercy on us!'

'On Daddy's yacht. He thinks I should,. He said it would broaden my experience. Especially if there are some really handsome hunks aboard! But don't tell him that.'

'And then?'

'Go on the stage, perhaps. I played Juliet in our school play. Have you seen Romeo and Juliet?'

'In its very first representation, at the Globe.'

'Wow! I can dance as well, you know. Would you like to see me dance?'

'Most verily.'

Polly put a tape into her ghetto-blaster, and as the music belted out, she gave it all she'd got.

'This is funky,' she shouted, ever the music.

'Monkey?' said Sir Edward, clapping his hands to his ears. 'Tis a measure fit for Barbary Apes!'

Polly stopped the tape.

'That's what Daddy says, more or less.'

'Would not you hear real music? Let me take my lute down from the wall. It has not been played these many years.'

He tuned it, struck a few chords, and began to sing.

Greensleeves was all my joy,
Greensleeves was my delight.
Greensleeves was my heart of gold,
And Who but my lady Greensleeves?

Polly joined in; she had learnt it at school.

'There! That was delightful, sweet Polly. Now, what miracle have you to show me next?'

'The Telly! There's a great late-night movie.'

She switched it on, and at once the announcer appeared on the screen.

'A puppet-show, by my troth!' Said Sir Edward. He walked round the back of the set, and peered at it in amazement. 'Yet where is he who pulls the strings of the marionette?'

'Nowhere,' said Polly, 'but it'd take too long to explain.'

She switched channels.

'Here's the late night movie,' she said.

In a Chicago apartment, a platinum-blonde chorus girl was filing her nails,

'A right comely wench,' said Sir Edward.

'Shhhh!' Said Polly, who was lost in the film.

The Tough Guy flung open the door.

'Two-time me, Sugar,' said the Tough Guy, 'and I'll push your kisser through the back of your head.'

The words were Greek to Sir Edward.

'Oh yeah, you big ape?' Said Sugar.

'Nobody calls me a big ape,' said the Tough Guy, seizing her violently by the wrist.

'Have a care, sirrah!' Said Sir Edward, springing to his feet.

'Says you, you big ape!' Sugar spat at him.

'You asked for it, Sugar. And now you're going to get it!'

He slapped her violently across the face.

It was more than old-world chivalry could stand.

'Have at you for a scurvy knave!' said Sir Edward, drawing his sword.

'No, Grandad, no!' screamed Polly. But she was too late.

Sir Edward ran the Tough Guy through with his sword. As it pierced the television screen, there was a crash of glass, and a tremendous flash and bang. All the lights went out. Backwards and forwards along his sword ran sparks and little blue flames. Then they died away.

'Are you all right, Grandad?' Screamed Polly.

'Darkness is come again!' He gasped.

'You've fused the lights, Grandad, That's why. You might have died.'

'Not a second time', said Sir Edward.

In the moonlight, his face was black with soot, and his hair stood on end.

'Would you like me to fix the lights? It wouldn't take long.'

'No, my dear. You look so pretty in the moonlight, just as my own dear Lady Alice did, so many years ago.'

'Let me clean you up a bit.'

So she did. They sat for a while hand in hand, happy simply to be together.

In the distance a cock crew. A pale streak appeared in the sky.

'My time is all but spent. 'tis nearly dawn.'

'Shall we ever meet again?' Asked Polly.

'Perhaps, in the land of shadows. I would like your portrait to hang in the Long Gallery,.'

'Me too', said Polly

'Before I go', said Sir Edward, 'I crave one last miracle.'

In the light of her torch, pink balls of paper raced round the inside of the toilet, and vanished forever.

She and Sir Edward mounted the grand staircase hand in hand, singing Greensleeves, but Sir Edward's hand melted from hers, and she climbed no further. He turned, doffed his hat, and bowed to her before disappearing altogether. Polly yawned hugely, and staggered off to bed.

Later that morning her father mended the fuses, and refused to believe her explanation. She found the lute leaning against the wall in the Long Gallery. It stood beneath the picture of Sir Edward Hawkesley, 1548-1602.

AUNTIE ZEINAB

In the old days, Ramallah Street was cool in the shadow of its houses and the palm trees that lined it, unless the sun was right overhead. Pavements hardly existed. One had to walk carefully to avoid occasional heaps of donkey dung, because the scavengers only cleared them away towards sunset. That was when men made their way to Souq Square for their evening coffee, glass of arak, and game of cards, or leant back in their chairs to talk about the way of the world.

But now it was very different. Huge blocks of masonry littered the road, and Auntie Zeinab picked her way carefully between them, holding her veil close to her face, to keep out the dust and the grit.

She was in no hurry - she had no evening meal to prepare. She used to make a delicious couscous, or lamb stewed with thyme - a wonderful aroma! But now that her husband and two sons were dead, she hardly cared whether she lived or died. She would cut herself a slice from a flat round loaf, and if there was a morsel of goat's cheese to go with it, so much the better. That was almost all the food she wanted.

Towards the end of the street was a faded green door with a rusty iron knocker. She rapped lightly on it. Nobody seemed to be watching, but she could not be too careful. She stood there with bowed head, and the patience all widows must learn. At last a quiet footfall reached the door. A young man with a neat moustache opened the door to her.

'I have come,' she said.

He wore a shirt open at the collar, and a black waistcoat above his sand-coloured denim trousers and sandals. He was her only contact with the organization.

She entered a little courtyard which had escaped the general bombardment. Plants grew in heavy stone jars ranged neatly round the walls, and, on a small terrace, vines screened a table from the noise and heat.

'The journey will not be comfortable,' he said, 'but it will not take long. You must remain totally silent and motionless, should problems arise. You can guess what might happen otherwise.'

She bowed her head in acceptance.

He led the way to a stable, where a dusty old car was standing. Its tyres were almost bald, and its number plates so dirty one could hardly read them.

He unlocked the boot, and held it open for her. She climbed awkwardly into it, being a rather bulky old woman, and lay down quietly on some dirty sacks. The lid of the boot closed. A little light filtered in through small chinks in the bodywork, but she could not see out through them. She did not even try.

The street door opened, the engine coughed into life, and the car jolted out into the road. It speeded up a little. Sometimes it swayed as it turned a corner, sometimes it braked, and sometimes the engine echoed, as if in a narrow alley.

In the darkness of the boot, memories came back to her. She remembered how, when she was sixteen, her parents had made an arranged marriage for her with Yusuf, her husband.

How handsome he was, with his red tasselled tarboosh, his dark green embroidered waistcoat, and his flowing trousers.

He had been all a husband could bc, God rest his soul, and she had borne him two fine sons, Hasan and Mehmet . She had always tried to be a good wife and mother, quiet, patient, and attentive to their needs. Until, that is, the Israeli troops drove into the village, and her husband and sons had gone out to confront them, and voice their anger. They had gone unarmed, that was beyond question; they had had no weapons. She never knew if their anger had turned to throwing stones. She was simply called to identify their bodies. They had been shot dead. Perhaps Hasan had turned to flee. He had been shot from behind.

Lonely and empty was her existence now. She had only ever worked as a housewife. But, after the bombardment, her house was an almost complete ruin. She had to fetch water from a distant tap, and buy flour from a man whose prices were too high and whose measures were too small.

She tried to patch the largest hole in the corner of her house, before bitter winds pinched her to the bone.

She had been robbed of all she possessed, save her name. They called her Auntie Zeinab, 'Auntie' being the courtesy title given to a woman of her age and situation.

And now came the time of reckoning.

Huddled in the boot of the car, she wondered whether it was making one direct journey or doubling back and forth, to disguise its route. Then the car stopped. Gates opened. It moved into cool shade inside a large empty warehouse, which had perhaps housed building materials. The driver helped her out of the boot. She was stiff after even that short ride - she was feeling her age – and she was given a chair to sit on facing a table with two more chairs. A gaunt man with a machine–gun stood on guard.

Then the driver blindfolded her. Two men entered the room and sat opposite her. She could only distinguish them by their voices,. One had the light, firm voice of a vigorous young man. The other's voice was deeper and heavier, as if weighed down with many sorrows and battle-scars.

'We got your message,' said the younger man. 'You have been blindfolded so that there is no risk of your recognising us again. It is in both our interests that it should be so.'

'I understand,' she said.

'Why is it, Auntie,' said the older man, 'that you want to see us?'

'My husband and sons were killed by the Israelies,' she said.

'We know that,' said the younger man, 'otherwise you would not have been brought here. Of course we sympathise with your great loss. They were all good men.'

'What else would you like to say?' said the older man.

'My life means nothing to me anymore,' she said. ' I want to give it to you. To the cause.'

'Let us be frank with you,' said the older man. 'You have no experience of fighting.'

'None, sir,' she said.

'Nor of explosives.'

'I could learn.'

'Weapons?'

'In the old days my husband and the boys would go out into the fields shooting pheasants,' she said. 'I would dress the pheasants for our meal, and clean and oil the guns, and put them carefully away till next time.'

'This is quite different,' he said.

'But I know what I must do. Go to a chosen place, bide my time, and then…'

'It sounds so easy, doesn't it, Auntie,' he said. 'As if any fool could do it.'

'My husband never thought me a fool,' she said.

'Of course not. Bu this is quite different. We have all the recruits we need. With each new atrocity, our numbers grow. But they are young. That is their special quality.'

'It could be my strength,' she said. 'Just look at me now. - '

She spread her arms expressively. 'An ordinary middle-aged woman. Men would not look twice at me. How different it once was!'

Her cheeks burnt as she remembered how, years ago, when she passed through Israeli check-points, the soldiers would undress her with their eyes, making obscene remarks, and subjecting her to all sorts of familiarities. She raged as she remembered it all.

'This is my only way to revenge my family. Please do not deny it me.'

He shook his head.

'No, Auntie, this is not for you. We always choose our targets for maximum effect. Every time we fail – it is not often - we give the enemy more heart. Our young fighters do not hesitate. But older people can have moments of hesitation and remorse. I'm sorry Auntie, but that is our final answer.'

She bowed her head, tears stinging her eyes, but she said nothing.

The two men retired and the gaunt man removed her blindfold. He led her across to the car, and helped her climb into the boot. Before he closed and locked it, he bent down to her.

'Don't tell anyone I gave you this,' he whispered, and pressed something into her grasp.

It was a hand grenade – she could tell at once, though it was wrapped in an old plastic bag.

''You know how it works?' he said.

'Yes, thank you,' she whispered.

During the jolting journey home she ran her finger over the grenade. It was the old 'pineapple' type, its surface ridged and squared, with a circular ring at the top attached to the pin. She knew that once she pulled the pin out and released the lever, it would explode in about five seconds. She hid it under her clothing, and got out of the vehicle.

Once safely inside her house, she unwrapped the grenade. It was covered all over with a thin film of dark grease, against rust, perhaps. She wiped it carefully clean, so that it smelt less of oil. Sniffer dogs might have spotted it, for all she knew. She replaced it in its plastic bag, and hid it under a loose stone in her courtyard. Now she could plan ahead.

It was absurd, it was unfair, it was ungrateful to trust only the young. She felt hurt, as if all her years of caring and experience counted for nothing. She thought of all the places where a grenade could be used to best effect.

A crowded school? Certainly not. There would be no soldiers there. A cinema where they were showing a popular film?

She would hurt more civilians than soldiers, and she would look completely out of place there Women of her age did not go to the cinema much.

A café? Only if a lot of soldiers were pesent. The more soldiers she killed the better – they would be more likely to include those who had killed her husband and sons. Was there a better place to explode her bomb?

Yes, a railway station, especially if a troop train was coming in. She would not look out of place in a railway station. And her own presence at a railway station would not seem extraordinary.

Tomorrow, at nine-fifteen, such a train was due.

She sat quietly in her room in the dark, as daylight faded into dusk. She slept briefly before dawn shaded into morning, and then she was ready.

She washed herself and put on the voluminous black dress which fitted her only where it touched, and uttered her morning prayers to Allah, the all-merciful. She went to the railway station. Sure enough, it was thronged with soldiers. There were civilians too, but that could not be helped.

She bought a ticket to the first station down the line. It cost her most of the little money she had. Then she climbed the footbridge to the main platform. A loud-speaker announced the train's imminent arrival. Under her dress she slipped her finger through the ring that held the safety–pin, She had practiced doing it often at home, even withdrawing the pin completely, and replacing it without releasing the lever.

She stood on the bridge in the bright morning sunshine. Directly below her was a throng of young soldiers, laughing and joking. She could have dropped the grenade then and there, but it was better to wait until the train came in. There would be more soldiers getting off the train, which would itself reflect the force of the blast. There was also a young officer, Lt. Dan Levy, who was waiting to meet his wife. He had been in charge of the soldiers at Souq Square. It was not a duty he enjoyed, but he was firm and efficient.

'Our job,' he told his men, 'is to preserve lives, if possible. Non-lethal force is our preferred option. We've got a tank in support, and you've got your loaded rifles, if the worst comes to the worst. But there must be no indiscriminate killing. If a mob gets out of hand, throwing stones, no-one is to fire until I give the order. The first shot goes over their heads, as a warning. Second shot, into the ground near their feet, as a final warning. If that doesn't stop them, pick out the ring-leaders. They'll be at the front, urging the others on. Those few lives may well be sufficient to prevent far worse bloodshed.'

The train came in, and slowed down. The best moment to drop the grenade was when soldiers started getting off the train.

Lt. Dan Levy stood there, smiling with his hands on his hips, waiting to meet his wife Miriam, and their little son. Auntie Zeinab pulled out the pin, and brought the grenade from under her dress. She had only to let it fall for it to explode.

Some soldiers on the train were crowding to the door, waiting to get off, but they stood back in the corridor to let Miriam and her son get off first.

The train stopped, and Miriam stepped out onto the platform, holding her little son. Auntie Zeinab could see their faces clearly. Miriam could so easily have been herself many years ago, when she was a bride; and the little boy could almost have been Hasan, her first-born son. Her heart turned over, and she could not drop the grenade. Now she understood why the secret organisation only entrusted its missions to young persons who would not know what a mother's love was really like.

She brought the grenade back under her clothing. It was not too late to push the pin back in. She tried to do it then and there, but her fingers would not let her. So be it; she could leave the station quietly and replace the pin outside. She had failed in her wish to avenge her own family, but could not carry the bloodshed any further.

Dan and Miriam were still on the platform - he was gathering up her luggage, and the train was about to start, when six soldiers came dashing across the bridge. They wanted to catch that train. Auntie Zeinab tried to back away from them, but they did not give her time.

'Out of the way, you old cow!' shouted one of them, barging into her as if it was a rugger game. She staggered back and almost lost her balance, and she dropped the grenade. It rolled a few feet away from her, and bounced, bounced, bounced noisily down the first steps to the platform. Then it fell through a gap in the structure.

Miriam must have heard it, because she raised her head to look. A grenade of that sort fragments into many sections – that is the purpose of its pineapple design – and wicked slivers of steel can easily travel one hundred feet. It exploded three feet above Miriam's head.

The bridge itself protected Auntie Zeinab from the main force of the blast. A stray sliver of steel nicked her arm just above the elbow, but she was otherwise unhurt She saw all of what the grenade had done. In the confusion, nobody thought fit to stop her. She turned away slowly, and left the station. Half an hour later , she was back home.

When night fell, she was still sitting, silent and motionless, in her little room. She had avenged her husband and family, in a way, but she had caused much more bloodshed.

That night the television news was full of the latest bombing outrage, carried out, people said, by a terrorist disguised as an old woman. There were immediate reprisals, of course, including a heavy bombardment of the quarter in which she lived. That night, and the night after, Auntie Zeinab wanted to live no longer, but the choice was not hers. It is very difficult to starve oneself to death. And she would never be given another grenade.

BEWARE THE VAFROUS ZAMOUSE

In the foyer of the Plaza Hotel, Keith Kennedy bumped into Viv Collins, so petite that she hardly came up to his elbow.

'I am most terribly sorry,' he said. 'Are you all right?'

'I don't mind being bumped into by strong handsome men,' she said roguishly. He was indeed well-made and good-looking. Viv, however, with her elfin charm, looked as if the lightest breeze could waft her away.

'It was just an accident,' said Keith defensively

'Of course,' said Viv. 'I didn't think you were vafrous enough to do it on purpose.'

'Vafrous!' He said in surprise. 'I'm here for the National Crossword competition, but I've never even heard of that word.'

'I'm here for it too,' she said. 'Vafrous comes from the Latin word vafer, meaning cunning or sly. You'll find it only in Webster's dictionary now.'

'It would score well in Scrabble,' he said.

'So would ZAMOUSE,' said Viv.

'That's a large animal, isn't it?' said Keith.

'Yes,' said Viv, 'It's a South African buffalo, with a peculiar fringing of the ears.'

'You really know your stuff!,' said Keith admiringly.

'I work in a science laboratory,' said Viv. 'So I use a lot of words most people wouldn't know.'

'I work in a complaints department,' said Keith, 'so I know a lot of words most people shouldn't use.'

A bell rang, and they took their places in the hall. Each competitor sat in his own little compartment, like a battery hen, so that he could not see what the person next door was writing. Three puzzles had to be solved in the morning session. Keith managed to finish the first two, and scored a total of 110.   Viv scored 112.

'I say,' said Keith, 'We've got almost the same score. Perhaps we were meant for each other.'

'Perhaps we were,' said Viv.

They still had almost equal scores by the end of the session, and had done well, though the winners had done better.

From that day onwards they rang each other every night, to complete their Times and Telegraph crosswords. They never won a prize – that takes luck – but they won each other's hearts. Six months later, they were married.

'Guess what I bought for our honeymoon,' said Keith at the airport. 'It's something special we can do together.'

'Something naughty?' said Viv hopefully.

'No, it's a Travel Scrabble set.'

'Can we have a game now, then?'

‘No, it's packed in my suitcase, unfortunately,‘ said Keith.

But fate played them a cruel trick. Their baggage got lost in transit.

‘I packed a specially gorgeous nightie for our wedding night,‘ said Viv tearfully.

‘We’ll just have to manage without,‘ said Keith. It worked surprisingly well.

Next morning they went shopping for basic items, including clothes.

‘Look,‘ said Viv, ‘there’s a Travel Scrabble set!‘

‘Yes, but it’s a Spanish set,‘ said Keith. ‘It won't have the same distribution of letters as an English one.‘

‘We'll just have to wait till we get home then,‘ said Viv. So they did.

Keith had hardly carried Viv over the threshold of their new flat when their lost baggage arrived back from the airport.

Soon they were sat in their kitchenette, with their Scrabble set. They were almost neck and neck, till Keith triumphantly laid down the word MUJZHIK. Worth 128 points, in that position.

‘That's not the way to spell it,‘ said Viv.

‘Are you challenging it?‘ said Keith.

‘I certainly am,‘ said Viv, ‘the word for a Russian peasant is MOUZHIK, or MUJIK. In English, either spelling will do.‘

‘So will MUJSHIK,‘ said Keith.

‘Bet you it won’t.‘

‘Bet you it will.‘

Viv riffled through a dictionary till she found the entry. The word only appeared as she had spelt it.

‘Ah,‘ said Keith, ‘but MUJZHIK was used last week in the Scrabble championship finals. Here it is. I kept the cutting.‘

‘Do you mean to tell me‘, said Viv, her voice rising in anger against the traitor that Keith now showed himself to be, “that you've been secretly swotting up on Scrabble words during our honeymoon?

‘Why not?‘ Said Keith.

‘Because – ‘ she groped for the right word – ‘you’re nothing but a MORMOPS!‘

‘Challenge!‘ Said Keith.

Viv seized the dictionary. ‘There you are,‘ she said, ‘MORMOPS. A repulsive leaf-nosed South American bat!‘

‘Doesn't count,‘ said Keith.

‘It's there, right in front of you,‘ said Viv.

‘Yes, but it's spelt with a capital M,‘ said Keith. ‘That makes it a proper noun. It doesn't count, in Scrabble.‘

‘it doesn't look as if our marriage counts for much, either,‘ said Viv, the tears streaming down her face.

‘But DIVORCE would,‘ said Keith, ‘especially if you put the V on a triple letter score.‘

Viv opened the kitchen cupboard, seized a saucepan, and threw it at him. It caught him on the ear.

‘That'll teach you to be so vafrous!‘ She shouted.

Keith grappled with her before she could find another missile..

It was their first lover's quarrel, and, like many lovers quarrels, it ended with them snug in each other's arms, under the duvet.

'Why should we quarrel? We could be a championship pair to beat the band,' said Keith.

So it turned out. In their first match, Viv came up with ZOOECIUM, "one of the cells or tubes which enclose the feeling zooids of Bryozoa," whatever they are, and in his turn he built across the Z to put down CAZIQUE, a local political boss in Spain or Latin America.

What does it matter who won the game? They rejoiced in each other's strengths, and lived happily ever after.

HAPPILY is a lovely seven-letter word. H and Y score four points each, and each P scores another three. Get it on a Triple Word Score if you can.

BISHOP CORVINO'S REVENGE

The pizza had only just come out of the oven, and was almost too hot to hold. The mozzarella cheese was still bubbling, and tomatoes. anchovies and olives made an appetizing pattern all over it. The man sitting on the pavement blew on the edge of it, and took a bite. Some of the cheese came away in trailing strings, like chewing-gum. He lay back contentedly against the low wall which separated the pavement from the beach. And looked up at Aunty Anna, who was waiting for his reaction. 'Father?' she said

'Mmph mmph hnnch hnnch nnnn,' he said, which is the Italian for "Too hot, but delicious.'

Aunty Anna stood there in her bare feet and shapeless black dress, one hand on her hip; her lined walnut face beamed, and with the back of her other hand she coyly seemed to push the compliment away.

A word of explanation is needed here. They were both using courtesy titles. 'Aunty' is a word applied in Southern Italy (and elsewhere) to any woman who has reached middle age; as to 'Father', she was old enough to be his mother. But he was a priest.

His black shirt may have been clean that very week; it was unbuttoned almost to the waist.

The sun beat down fiercely on the Via Varese. A strong smell of garlic from the fishing boats was mixed with the tang of the salt air and the stink of fish. It was as heady as a cocktail - better than the Viale di Genoa, where there was more than a hint of drains below, and the endless lines of washing shut out the midday sun above.

The street was almost deserted. Most people had gone home for their midday meal. A few fishermen dozed in the shade of their boats, hauled well up the beach.

From an upstairs window, where the shutters had been partly closed to keep out the heat, but not enough to keep in the savoury smell of mussels cooking in olive oil with garlic and herbs, came the sound of a cheap radio. A tenor with a small orchestra was singing popular songs.

The man in the street waved a slice of pizza in time to the melody as he went on eating. The rest of the pizza lay in his lap; he had a handful of olives in his left hand. He was not expecting a black limousine to come quietly down the street and stop beside him. It had hardly any business to be there, since the main traffic kept to the Corso Garibaldi half a mile away. When he saw who was in the back seat, he sprang to his feet, still clutching the pizza.

'Please tell me', said the chauffeur in a peaked cap, 'the way to San Matteo's church.'

The man on the pavement muttered some directions, with indications of his hands of a turn to the left, and then to the right. Italians are not naturally laconic, but he had his mouth full.

'And also to the house,' said the distinguished passenger in the rear of car, of Father Massari.'

The fishermen in the shade of their boats began to grin, and Aunty Anna cackled like a hen which has just laid an egg.

'Why, Monsignor,' said the man on the pavement, '`I have to admit… Father `Massari… is me.'

There was a long pause, during which an iceberg seemed to surface in the sparkling waters of the bay.

'You!' said the Bishop.

Father Massari coughed discreetly., transferring two olives to his fist.

'You,' continued the Bishop, 'a member of the Holy Church, dress like an urchin, and adopt the habits of the alleys?'

Father Massari turned a darker colour beneath his deep tan, and let the olive stones trickle from his hand into the gutter.

'Is this the way you lead your flock?'

'I try, Monsignor,' said the priest, 'to be close to their hearts, to understand them at their own level.'

'Humility,' said the Bishop, 'is a great virtue. We remember with joy the example of our late Pope John. But –' here he looked witheringly up and down - 'cleanliness is another.'

'Today I have been working with them and for them, Monsignor.'

'In bare feet, I suppose A true disciple of the church walks at least in the shoes of the Fisherman. All I can say is that your discipline is sadly lacking.'

'And all I can say,' shouted the priest, losing his temper, is –

Here followed an extremely colourful expression, much used in the locality. It loses a lot in translation, and might be unfamiliar even then.

A great guffaw went up from the spectators. Monsignor Corvino moved his face slowly back inside the car like a snail retreating into its shell. The limousine drove noiselessly away.

All the way back to the Bishop's Palace thoughts buzzed round and round in his head. His first were of outrage, that an ordinary priest should dare to talk to him like that.

Next came the sting of ingratitude. He had heard many tales of Father Massari's work in the slums. Where so many priests had tried and failed.

But apart from the achievements among the poor and the criminal classes, there were rumours of certain irregularities, which had caused him to make his exceptional visit. Bishop Corvino wished to discuss them. Not with reproaches, but with reasoning. Some of the Bishop's colleagues, behind his back, called him 'the Crab', because of his supposedly sour behaviour. His mouth turned down in a familiar expression when he thought of it. But there was a happier explanation. He might, he thought, have been called 'the Crab' because he did not tackle things head on, but preferred a more sideways approach, with tact and no more harshness than was necessary. He felt himself misunderstood, for, as he approached the age of 65, he had learned more wisdom than people gave him credit for.

He thought back to the days when he was young in the priesthood, full of vigour and enthusiasm. Nobody called him 'the Crab' then, but 'Guido;' strange that nobody used his Christian name to him now.

He remembered especially the terrible month of August 1943, when the air raids hammered Milan. The church and the school he worked at were almost in the shadow of a munitions factory. For day after day they escaped devastation almost by a miracle. But at last their luck ran out.

He was too late to drag all the children to safety from the burning building; the front page of the national papers carried a picture of him in his torn cassock, standing amidst the rubble with the body of a little girl cradled in his arms, and the tears streaming down his cheeks.

As a picture of sorrow and suffering it was unforgettable, but it brought him the mild reproach of a wise bishop.

'Your courage did great credit both to yourself and to us, Guido,' he said. 'but your sorrow and anguish are not what the church expects you to express. When others feel grief beyond their power to sustain, to whom should they turn? The church. In a world of human frailty, who should display inexhaustible calm and strength? The church. Whatever your inward sorrows, Guido, it is your outward tranquility you must offer to others. It is so inside the Confessional; it is so in the world beyond.'

'But I am only human, my Lord,' said the young Guido.

'Of course,' said the Bishop. 'At times you will despair and at times you will be moved to wrath. But it must always be controlled.'

Guido never forgot those words. It seemed as if something died inside him, yet from that moment on he gained new powers of will. He kept the newspaper cutting locked away in a drawer. Whenever he looked at it he saw himself not as a hero, but someone who had displayed his weaknesses.

'If I had shown myself firm, if I had repaired my cassock;', he thought, 'how much more I should have served the purposes of God.'

There followed many moments of earnest prayer.

Over the hours that followed the incident on the Via Varese Bishop Corvino gave much thought to the problems of Father Massari. He could not get them out of his mind for, if the truth were told, there was mush more of him inside the Bishop than people might have supposed. Even at his sternest he felt himself torn between the rules and authority which were so important in a shifting and dangerous world, and the freedom of thought and action which divine inspiration sometimes suggested.

In Father Massari's case his experience warned him that the matter could not be left unresolved. If he could be taught the lesson he himself had learned when the bombs fell, it would give him a maturity which his impulsive nature needed. He could summon Father Massaari before him on a disciplinary charge, and pronounce a severe reprimand upon him. But to the people of the slums it would seem a hollow gesture and a symbol of officiousness, Father Massari would become a martyr in their eyes.

If, however, he let the matter slide, Father Massari would become a hero, free to do what he liked. It would be bad for his soul and his ministry. Besides, the people had laughed at him, and to laugh at the Bishop in his authority was to laugh at the Holy Church itself. He needed a course of action which would make his point in a way the local inhabitants understood. As he stood at the window of the Bishop's Palace the sunlight faded from the formal garden in front of him. An early autumn wind swayed the turning leaves on the trees, and the sky turned a steely grey. A storm was coming. He knew at once what he must do.

On the next Sunday morning, when his congregation had left the nine o'clock Mass, Father Massari left San Matteo's church and stood on the pavement looking down the street. They started to scurry away in the pouring rain. The rain hurried pieces of paper and rubbish along the gutters and into the gurgling drains.

There was no traffic at all. So he was surprised to see, coming towards him down the centre of the road, the black limousine with the distinguished passenger. This time, however, the Bishop was sitting on the front seat beside the driver.

"I've got my shoes on, at any rate,' thought Father Massari to himself, and buttoned his cassock up properly. The car was approaching him from the side, as all good Crabs should do. It seemed, oddly enough, as if the Bishop was actually sniling at him. He could not understand why.

The car suddenly picked up speed, and swerved towards the edge of the pavement.

'It cannot be going to run me down1' thought Father Massari, jumping back from the edge of the pavement. But he was too late. The car came within one foot of the kerb, and swerved away again. Ir entered a deep puddle with a whoosh which sent muddy water all over the priest.

Some of the local fishermen, in their Sunday clothes, uttered a hearty guffaw, and Aunty Anna, in her best black lace headscarf, split her face in a grin.

Bishop Corvino saw it all as he turned round in his seat, and Father Massari saw in his quiet smile something of forgiveness and reconciliation. The Bishop raised his hand, in gtreeting, and the priest inclined his head in a respectful bow.

Bishop Corvino returned to the Bishop's Palace in a high good humour. The incident was now closed; there was no need for any official charge to be filed for the initial insolence, and the punishment had fitted the crime in a way the local people understood.

There was one other thing which mattered hardly at all, yet gave him some personal satisfaction. He had had his revenge.

COPY CAT

It was just as well I kept my mouth shut while the Judge was passing sentence, or he might have made it twice as long.

'Ronald Spratt,' he began.

How I hated that name! It took me back to the days when I was a snotty-nosed little kid in Mangle Street, and all the other kids ganged up on me, calling me 'Runny Ronnie.' I sometimes wet my bed – and they ran after me chanting

'Ronnie Spratt Peed on his cat,'

which was ridiculous. We didn't even have a cat.

What I had, though, was a drunken father who liked nothing better than to take off his belt and then flay the living daylights out of me, when he got home from the pub. All my mother did - she was as weak as water – was to whisper,

'Try not to upset your father, Ronnie.'

When I grew big and strong, - I was surprised when it happened – the other kids left me alone. So did my father, when I stood up to him. Before that, though, Mrs. Furniss was the only bright spot in my life.

She worked at the Public Library, and found me gorgeous story-books with knights in shining armour, princesses, and dragons.

She gave me a nice colouring book, too, with a set of crayons. I coloured them beautifully, she said.

This was where my career really started, you see. When I was nine, she took me to the Art Gallery where they had a children's group, and again I did really well. At first I signed my little pictures 'Ronnie', but then it became 'Roland', after one of those knights in armour. For a surname I chose 'Spurgeon,' which sounded good.

'Roland Spurgeon' was a name to make any painter proud.

'Ronald Spratt', repeated the Judge, - perhaps he thought I wasn't paying attention – 'you have pleaded guilty to seven acts of fraud. For large sums of money you sold faked paintings with effortless ease – I thought, gripping the brass rails of the dock so tightly that my knuckles showed white. I went to huge trouble to obtain suitable old canvases, frames, and pigments, and I studied the techniques of all the artists I chose to copy. I was a natural copycat, it turned out.

Not for me the great dollops of paint which Rembrandt used so well, or the whirling circular brush-strokes of Van Gogh's Starry Night. But I loved the tiny meticulous details of the 'School of Van Eyck,' as they called it. I was certainly an assiduous pupil, even if my pictures were several centuries too late. I could have earned six-figure sums forging the major artists, but it was too risky. I got £40,000 for The Spinning Wheel, a woman with a gentle smile working away in a serene Dutch interior. That was 'School of Van Eyck,' as well.

'There is no hope,' continued the Judge,' of you ever repaying your victims. You squandered every penny.'

When he said that, I hid my face in my hands. He thought it was remorse, but I was laughing.

'Squandered? I made the most of every penny. If you'd been born and bred in Mangle Street, you'd rejoice in what money could do. It brought me style and status. I rubbed shoulders with the smart set, and made love to beautiful women. Silk gowns by night, and silk pyjamas at dawn. When the money ran out, I simply painted more pictures.

'It is to your credit,' said the Judge, 'that you made a full and frank admission of all your offences to the police.'

I was bent almost double in the dock then, my shoulders shaking with laughter, not remorse. Occasionally, when art critics questioned the genuineness of my paintings, my lawyer threatened to sue them for defamation, and they backed down.

Some galleries had doubts about some pictures. They described them in their catalogues now as 'possibly' the 'School of Van Eyck.'

Sometimes I played the innocent, and refunded some of the purchase price 'for the sake of good business relations.' But no gallery ever blew the whistle on me; they would have had to admit that they had been taken for a ride.

It wasn't until a police officer came to my studio to serve a summons on me for speeding - my sports car flew like a bird - that he saw some of my unfinished Old Masters with the paint still wet upon them. And that was that.

'The least sentence I can pass upon you,' said the Judge, 'is two years' imprisonment.'

Surely not! I hadn't committed any violent crimes, and my victims hadn't lost any sums they couldn't afford. But the Judge had not finished yet.

'Two years imprisonment,' he continued, 'of which you will serve the first year in prison. The rest will be suspended for two years.'

That was much better. Into the cells I went, but one week later I was transferred to Kerningford open prison. My cell window there faced south, overlooking the estuary, and it could hardly have suited me better. Mr. Collinge, the Prison Governor, allowed me to have painting materials.

'So long as you don't go painting any more Old Masters,' he said, 'all right?"

Why did I turn to forgery? Because people wouldn't buy my own stuff. I liked my pictures to be bright and simple and direct, like the story-books I'd seen. I got a small grant to go to Art College when I was sixteen, but my face just didn't fit in there at all. I hated pictures of drab ugly people – especially if they'd got no clothes on! – and I hated ugly abstract pictures, and clever-clever stuff where the artists glued drab, ugly bits and pieces from their dustbin onto their canvases.

I'd probably have been thrown out of Art College anyway, but I was caught doing an Un-still Life - , get my meaning? With a beautiful model named Enid. 'Eager Enid,' she was known as. She got kicked out too, and it was years before I saw her again. But I went on painting because I had to, and tried to make my stuff as good as the minor Masters, whom I copied and copied. I began to feel as if I was standing in their shoes, doing the public a favour by producing pictures I think those artists would have liked. The fact that I got good money from it was an added bonus, but most of all it was the joy of the pictures themselves.

Inside Kerningham open prison, I made the most of what was available. So my next pictures were estuary landscapes. Reeds, mud flats and waterfowl. In the cold silvery light of winter, with a melancholy charm of their own. Few people wanted to buy them even when I was better known, but I had another unexpected turn of fortune. I painted Jack Grimble's portrait.

Jack was in for burglary, and he had a face which combined cunning, charm and intelligence. (He had a brother working in the media, where these qualities are evidently invaluable.)

'There you are, Jack,' I said, 'that shows your strength of character. You could go in for politics.'

He was tickled pink with it, and showed it to everybody. Including Mr. Collinge, who sent for me.

'We don't often have people of your talents in here,' he said. 'Would you like to give some talks about painting?'

So I did. I gave a weekly lecture to the lads, and always included a nude for them, as a bonus.

I told them some racy stories of artists and their models. Mr. Collinge sat in on some of them, smoking his pipe, and he chuckled as much as anyone when I told them about the great French artist Corot.

'He painted two and a half thousand pictures in his lifetime,' I said, 'of which almost eight thousand are currently in the United States.' They loved it.

The time passed almost too quickly, till the prison gates closed behind me for the last time. The spring sunshine was cheerful, but my prospects weren't. I was given a damp little flat on the top floor of Gubbin Heights, with cracked windows, bare bulbs in the ceiling, and a tenant in the flat next door who shared all his favourite music with me, at full blast. I had practically no money, and you can guess why. I'd spent most of it on artists' materials. Old habits die hard. I rang my old friends for help, but they put the receiver down on me. One day all I had to eat was an untouched prawn sandwich someone had left in a bus shelter.

I drifted down to the waterfront, where a hefty woman was dragging her chinless husband away from the prom, to stop him looking at pretty girls. I did a lightning sketch of them on my drawing pad, and showed it them They burst out laughing, and gave me a fiver for it. For the rest of the afternoon I dashed off lightning sketches, of courting couples, babies in prams, and the donkey rides. I was onto a good thing.

By the end of the day I'd earned seventy quid, and within a month I found a much nicer flat, overlooking Whitewell Park.

They had a fairground there every summer, with fairy lights and garish neon signs which cried out for colour painting. Acrylic paint caught the mood beautifully.

My best piece was The Merry-go-round. On the left you saw a horse and rider, and they were static. But as you looked from left to right, the figures stretched into a blur of movement. As a critic later said. You could almost hear the music of the carousel.

This was my 'Neon period.' I got £75 each for them from art galleries, with the hope of more as they became better known. I was happy creating something of value in its own right. I was starting to pay my way.

Then disaster struck. My flat was burgled, and stripped completely bare. I'd had the sense to insure it, and put in a claim. But my story hit the headlines, and the insurers learnt that I had a criminal record. They repudiated liability.

'What for?' I asked.

'You've got criminal convictions,' they said.

'Not now,' I protested.

'Makes no difference,' they said. 'You didn't disclose your criminal record, and that invalidates your policy.'

'That's a breach of my human rights,' I protested. I've served my time, and I'm entitled to put it all behind me.'

But they were adamant. I'd been in prison and not told them. That made all the difference.

All I'd got now were the clothes I stood up in. But Alexander Berman, of the Aurora Gallery, sent me £100 for an estuary painting he'd just sold, so that night I dined in style. I bought myself a good bottle of red wine, a tin of corned beef, and a sliced loaf. I laid the table with a copy of the colour supplement of the Sunday Times, no less, and prepared for a banquet.

There came a knock at the door. I opened it, and came face to face with a burglar. It was Jack Grimble. (I drew his portrait in Kerningford, you may remember.)

'So you're in,' he said.

'Of course I'm in,' I said. 'But the last time I was out, someone burgled this flat, and cleared me out. I suppose you know all about that?' I said accusingly.

'Yeah, as a matter of fact,' he said. 'The two as did it, were boasting about it down the pub. When I heard who they'd done over, I thought I'd pay you a call.'

'Just tell me who they were,' I said. 'I'll sort them.'

'Too late,' he said. 'They sold the stuff and spent it on booze.'

'All right,' I said grudgingly. 'Help yourself to a sandwich.'

'No thanks,' he said. 'But I've got some good news for you.'

'Not the Royal Academy,' I said. 'I didn't submit anything this year.'

'Better than that,' he said, laughing, 'it's the Telly.'

'Haven't got one,' I said. 'They pinched it.'

'My brother's in television,' said Jack, 'did I ever tell you?'

'Yes, I remember.'

'Good,' he said. 'He saw the portrait you'd done of me, and I told him about your talks to us in the nick. Full of jokes. Great stuff.'

'That's nice,' I said.

'Anyway,' they're looking for a new Arts programme. Not too expensive, not too highbrow.'

So I went to see his brother, and that's how Copycat was born. I demonstrated the styles of Rembrandt one week, Van Gogh the next, and so on. It really went down a bomb. You see, I wasn't talking down to my audience. I was giving them everything I'd got. And they loved it. I chucked in a few nudes as well. That did the ratings no harm, I can tell you!

The programme ran for six whole years and made a media person out of me. I couldn't walk down the street without posh restaurateurs throwing themselves at my feet. 'Do come and dine at L'Escargot d'Or,' they'd say, 'so long as we can take a photo of you enjoying our food,'

'Done!' I said.

I can't remember when I last paid for a meal after that. I appeared on television commercials, and got paid a mint of money for doing it. But the nice letters I got pleased me more than anything. People said I'd made Art really interesting, and some went in for painting too.

I gave talks to students, and judged competitions. Even at the Royal Academy they accepted me for what I was, because I didn't pretend to be anything else.

I'd had enough of the wine women and song, but Enid took me up –She organized me marvelously well, so that we became a reliable and highly respectable couple. But she could never persuade me which offers to refuse. I'd been rather overdoing it, opening a gallery at one place, and lecturing at another, and judging a competition somewhere else. If they'd ever invented a thirty-six hour day, I'd have been their best customer.

I came down to breakfast one morning, to open the mail, but I couldn't do it. My hand felt like a bundle of wet rags, as if it didn't belong to me. I could flap my arm around a bit, but that was all. I tried to call Enid, but the wet rags got into my mouth as well, like after five drinks too many, know what I mean?

I'd had a stroke.

Enid turned up trumps then. She nursed me devotedly, giving me a special hug when I managed to do things right. She got me to practice my words over and over again till they came out more right than wrong. I made an almost full recovery, except that I couldn't paint any more. Still, my eyes and brain were as good as ever. So I could judge competitions and open fairs as well. On bad days she worked out what I wanted to say, and said it herself on my behalf. So everyone was happy.

But it took a lot out of her. Her cheeks grew hollow, and her hair turned grey, but she never complained, right up to the day she had her heart attack, and was taken from me.

I'd just got home from her funeral when I had my second stroke. I'd been warned it might happen –I'm just glad she wasn't there to see it. She'd have been so miserable, after all she'd done for me.

I hadn't got her to look after me any more, and the people they sent to look after me were useless. So they moved me into this hospice, where I got round-the-clock treatment.

'Don't fret yourself,' said Nurse Cadwallader - she's one I get on best with - 'and don't expect too much. Above all, don't go losing your temper.

It worked fine, till the day she said there was a police Inspector to see me.

'Shall I bring him in?' she said. "If he says you robbed the Central Bank last Saturday, I'll give you a perfect alibi.'

She was good with me like that.

'Here he is,' she said, ushering him in. 'I'll leave the door ajar, so if you want anything, just give me a shout.'

The Inspector came in, and placed something carefully against the wall at the foot of the bed.

'It's about a forged picture,' he said.

I wanted to tell him that I'd already served my sentence for that, years ago, but my mouth was full of wet rags again.

'What?' I mumbled.

'Someone was trying to sell one of your pictures for

£15,000,' he said, 'and we want to know if it's a fake.'

He unwrapped it carefully, and stood it on a chair where I could see it in a good light.

It was the Merry-go-Round, after all these years. It did my heart good to see it, but there was something funny about it.

'There,' I said 'there.' I pointed to the signature, and shook my head. It was signed Roland Spurgeon, all right, except that the 'Roland' had a 'w' in the middle.

'it's spelt wrong, is it sir?' said the Inspector.

I nodded. The wet rags wouldn't let me say more.

'Anything else, sir?'

I looked at the picture again. The lighting was right, with the fairy lights and the glaring neon, but – ah, that was it. The forger had put in a little girl at the rear, watching the merry-go-round with wide eyes. She was very striking, but it wasn't my picture. I shook my head violently again.

'You didn't paint this picture yourself, sir? You're quite certain about that?'

I nodded violently, and uttered a loud groan.

Nurse Cadwallader returned in a flash, and could see at a glance how things were

'You'll have to leave, now, sir,' she said to the Inspector.

All right,' he said. 'If I come back tomorrow, might I hope to take a statement from you then?'

'Ring before you come, sir,' she said to him, 'in case it isn't possible.'

‘Certainly,’ said the Inspector, ‘I’ll leave the picture here for the moment, if I may.’

He stood it on a table where I could see it clearly.

‘I’ll be back in a moment to give you an injection,’ said Nurse Cadwallader, and she ushered the Inspector out,

I lay there looking at the picture. It really was outrageous - it really was OUTRAGEOUS –

Careful, now, I didn’t want to have another stroke, so I lay back and closed my eyes, Then a thought came to me. Even though a forgery, that picture was pretty damned good. It captured exactly the garish atmosphere of my neon pictures. Besides - this made me smile - it was ironic that I, who had launched my career by forging other people’s pictures, should now myself be deemed worth forging.

I had only forged minor masters myself, at one with the painters I so much loved and admired.

I felt tired now, more tired than I had ever been before, and I closed my eyes as the world slipped away from me. But I was sure that, when Nurse Cadwallader came back and found me, there would be on my face an expression of radiant joy.

DIVERSION

Elderly Miss Farnworth was pedalling her way quietly home from the shops. A little blue van pulled up ahead of her. The words CROKER'S FOG DISPERSAL UNITS were painted on its sides.

Something to do with Radar, she thought.

'Excuse me, missus,' said the driver, 'am I right for the Airport?'

'Certainly,' she said. 'Keep straight on to the roundabout, and then take the second turning on the left. You can't miss it.'

'Thanks, love,' said the driver, and drove on.

She had just mounted her cycle again when she heard the squeal of brakes. Three children ran into the road after a ball; the van swerved and missed them, but it mounted the pavement, smashed through a wall, and stopped. The driver's door sprang open on the impact; his legs were crushed in the wreckage. By the time the ambulance arrived Miss Farnworth had aged several years.

Her health had never been strong; she had retired from teaching at 56. For months after the accident she kept to her house. One October afternoon, however, she looked at herself in the mirror.

This is nonsense, Kitty, she said to herself. We can't allow ourselves to be enslaved by the past.

She put on her hat firmly and mounted her bicycle. The trees in the park glowed wine and gold.

She came to the wall, so well repaired, you would never know it had been damaged. She ran her hand over the perfectly matching stones. A police car drew up.

'Is everything all right, madam?' asked a police officer. 'You seem to be looking for something.'

'I was thinking how well they had repaired the wall after the accident,' she said.

'Accident,' madam?

'Yes, here in April. A van crashed through it. The driver was badly injured.'

'No, madam,' said the constable. 'There's been no accident. I'm in the Traffic Division. I know every serious accident we've had here in the last three years. - Are you all right, madam?'

'I don't know,' she faltered.

'You look a bit peaky, madam. Should I run you home? My colleague can bring your bike.'

'No', she said. 'It's all right, really it is. I just thought I saw the accident with my own eyes, and now it seems there never was one.'

'Well, madam,' said the constable cheerfully, 'it's nice to have one accident too few!'

He drove away.

She felt her forehead; no fever there. The sunlight was real, and the children's laughter in the park was real. She was just mounting her cycle again when a little blue van pulled up ahead of her. The words CROKER'S FOG DISPERSAL UNITS were painted on the sides. Same van, same driver.

'Excuse me, missus,' he said, 'am I right for the Airport?'

She dismounted, and leant her bicycle carefully against the wall.

'Let me think,' she said, and rubbed her hand against the van. Real dirt smudged off on her.

'No,' she said, 'you're going the wrong way. You'll have to turn round.'

'That's funny,' said the young driver. 'I was told to keep straight on, and then ask again.'

'Yes,' she said hastily, 'but there's been a diversion. You'll have to go back to the lights, then left along the dual carriageway as far as the Fire Station, and then left again. It's about 6 miles.'

'The signpost said 3 miles,' he replied.

'Yes, but that's not counting the diversion. You'll have to go back, really you will. You WILL. Can't you understand?'

Her pale hand strayed to her face.

'Right, love,' he said, 'if you say so.'

He backed the car into the mouth of a side road, to go back the way he had come. She closed her eyes in a brief prayer of thankfulness. Then she heard the squeal of brakes. Three children ran into the road after a ball.

A petrol tanker, surging towards them, could never have stopped in time, but swerved to the left, and gashed its side against a bus shelter. Petrol flooded into the road around the Croker's van. The young driver tried to run away, but it was too late. The petrol went up with a whoosh, and for a moment he seemed to dance like a little puppet in the heart of the flames.

The damaged wall has since been repaired.

Miss Farnworth has never been out on her bicycle since that day, which is hardly surprising.

DOORS

Raymond Rockwell kicked open the front door of the cottage, because nobody answered to his knock. He was not a patient man. He looked down at an old woman who was sat by the fireside. It was a poorly furnished room; the table and chairs were of cheap wood, and bunches of herbs hung from the ceiling.

Ray moved forward till his beer belly was resting on the table, and struck it with a heavy fist.

"Where's me money?" he demanded.

Old Mother Hopkin, as she was known in the village, looked up at him. Her thin face, framed by straggling white hair, showed no fear.

"What money?" she said.

'THE money," he said, "all thirty-five thousand quid of it. Owin' on your cottage."

She carefully set down her teacup.

"I don't owe you any money," she said. "I don't even know who you are."

"I'm Ray Rockwell," he said, the chin jutting forward in his bullying face. "Ray's the name, and Raise the money's the game."

Even she had heard of Ray Rockwell, the ruthless landlord and property developer.

"I only owe the money to Mr. Francis Good," she said. "He lent it me."

"And I bought up all his assets," said Ray, with a leering smile on his beefy face, "So it's me you owe the money to. And I want me money NOW."

"I haven't got it," she said. "He promised I wouldn't have to pay till I could afford it."

"That was then, and this is now," he said. ``Yesterday was the date for foreclosure on your mortgage. That leaves me with no alternative."

"Doesn't it?" she said quietly.

"No, or you don't know me. As I said," he grinned. "I'm Ray Rockwell. Isn't that enough?"

She drew back. "Couldn't you give me some time?" she faltered.

"Sure," he said, with the grin of a lion at feeding time at the zoo. "Half an hour."

"To find thirty-five thousand pounds?"

"No, to get out. Shouldn't take you that long to put your bits and pieces into a bag."

"And then?"

'The bulldozer moves in. Flattens your cottage, and makes way for a decent new development."

"You can't flatten Rose Cottage," she said. "It's been here for four hundred years. It's a Grade II listed building."

"Can't I?" he said laughing. "I know all the right people. In the right places. I've got the Power."

"But suppose I had the Knowledge?" she replied.

"Nah," he said derisively. "Suppose – just suppose – a heavy lorry crashed into your cottage - by accident, of course – and half demolished it. The local authority wouldn't lift a finger to protect the wreckage. That's when Rockwell Developments moves in, to clear the mess away, and replace it with something much bigger and better. Like a Road-house and Casino. It's just what a dead-end dump like this needs."

"This is a protected area of outstanding natural beauty. The local authority would never allow it."

"They'd allow ME," he said, his pride and arrogance making him swell out like a bull-frog. "My money talks."

"Damn you to hell," she said, bitterly.

"Bollocks," he said, "There's no hell, and I don't believe in damnation."

She fought for words.

"A plague upon you, then," she said.

"Not under the National Health, love, no," he laughed. "I'll be back in half an hour. Best be ready."

He strode away, and gave orders to his demolition crew, who were waiting outside with their bulldozer. When he came back, she was still sitting at her fireside. On the table stood a black candle and a Celtic dagger with its point towards the door.

The candle was lit, and a pewter tankard containing some hot strong-smelling potion was beside it.

"Hey-up!" he said. "What's all this? Are you supposed to be a witch, or something?" He had heard tales about her in the village.

"And supposing I was?" she said.

"Oo-er, I am frightened!," he said, as if talking to a small child. "I'll cast a spell on YOU," he said, and raising two fingers obscenely towards her, he made the sign of the cross.

"Itchy-witchy, silly bitchy," he said, and spat in her face.

That was a mistake. She dashed the hot liquid in his face – it tasted foul, and made his eyes sting. He staggered back with a cry, while she pronounced a spell of her own. Her voice had a cracked intensity, her eyes seemed blacker than ever, and her fingers more like claws.

"By the powers of hell and death,
You shall draw your final breath.
Go through one door, and you'll find
You'll see nothing, as if blind.
One more door, and there's no sun.
Then your days are truly done."

While he stood wiping the foul fluid from his face, she got up and left quietly by the front door of the cottage, carrying her few belongings in a suitcase . There was a gypsy settlement a mile away; they would be glad to welcome her, she knew.

Ray stepped outside the cottage and gave a nod to the bulldozer, which rammed the side of the building. It collapsed, and Ray stepped into the back of the room, looking with approval at the damage.

"That'll teach her," he said. Rather than climb back over the rubble, he turned to the back door. It proved surprisingly stiff to open; he had to put his shoulder to it violently. The door creaked, but did not open at first. "Another one should do it," he said, and this time the door flew open. Some mist floated into the room.

"That's funny," he thought, "it was quite sunny just now."

He stepped outside. The mist was cold, and so thick that he could not even see the bulldozer. Then he heard shouting, the sound of bullets, and the hooves of a galloping horse, which bore down on him out of the fog.

"Who goes there?" shouted a rider, who was dressed as a Roundhead officer of the Civil War.

"Only me," said Ray, who could think of no better answer. He had slagged his way through history lessons at school, and did not know that Rose Cottage stood on the site of one of the skirmishes in the Civil War.

"Art thou one of the King's men?"

"What king?" said Ray. He belonged, of course, to the reign of Queen Elizabeth.

"Then thou art one of Cromwell's men," said the rider, drawing his sword and slashing at Ray's shoulder. It cut deep into his arm. "So DIE!"

He raised his sword again, and was about to strike a blow which would have taken Ray's head off, when there was a loud explosion, and a cannon-ball struck the rider full in the chest, so that he fell from his horse, a dead man. Ray, spattered by his blood, hobbled away as fast as he could into the mist. There were shouts on all sides, and volleys of musket-shots, and occasional glimpse of soldiers engaged in hand-to-hand combat. But the sounds died away, and Ray paused for breath. He had to, because years of corporate development – his beer-belly! – made him unused to active exercise, and he was weak from the wound to his arm. He stood alone in the mist and silence, but the mist cleared, and he saw a street of half-timbered houses. He ran to the back of the nearest one, where a door was ajar. He found himself in a very old-style kitchen, with no sign of a gas oven or electric stove anywhere. He tried to open an interior door, but it was wedged with the hand of a corpse lying flat on its back. All he could see was that blue hand. He made his way to the front door. It opened without difficulty, but there was an X painted on the front of it. He did not know that this was a sign of the visitation of the Plague. Two planks of wood were nailed diagonally across its opening, to make it difficult for people to get in or out.

He squeezed under them, and stepped out into a street which stood empty under a full moon. The houses stood so close together that a man might lean out of his upstairs window and shake the hand of a man in the house opposite.

There were no longer any sounds of guns or voices, but only a horse's hooves and a cart on the cobbled street. As it drew nearer he could hear an old man crying "Bring out your dead!" The cart was carrying several corpses. He stood there till the man grew level with him, and their eyes met.

"Bring out your dead," the old man insisted in a hoarse voice. The eyes in his hollow face were deep-set and rheumy. Ray's knees grew weak beneath him, and he collapsed onto the ground. When he came to, he could feel the jolting of the cart beneath him. He was lying on top of other corpses. The jolting ceased; the cart had left the cobbles, and was following deep ruts into a large open field, where the plague pit was. Ray tried to roll off the cart, but another body had wedged him in. The cart stopped, and the man tilted it violently, so that, one after another, the bodies slid off it and into the pit. Ray could do nothing to help himself. He was shaken and shocked by his fall into darkness.

"I'm alive!" he tried to shout, but it only came out as a feeble croak. He made another desperate effort. "I'M –" he began, but a heavy shovel-full of earth blocked his mouth. "I'M – " he tried again, but another shovel-full fell on his head, and a third one covered it over.

There are few worse fates than being buried alive, but being buried alive in a plague-pit is one of them. The witch's curse came true; he suffered hell and damnation, and the plague was upon him.

NO ROOM AT THE HOSTEL

The car ground to a halt near the kerb, and the lights went out.

'Damn it!' said Jack. 'That's all we need.'

He tried to start it again. The engine coughed hoarsely. The headlights flickered like the eyes of an elderly invalid, and went out again. That's what comes of buying a clapped-out old banger at the airport, dirt cheap.

'It's only got to get us to Glasgow,' Jack had said. 'Any more is a bonus.'

Famous last words. The woman in the passenger seat sat silent. Only the whites of her eyes showed in her jet-black face. This was as nothing compared to the great civil war massacre, and a frantic escape across the desert. He placed his hand reassuringly on hers, and stepped from the car.

'Can you tell me the way to the nearest garage?' he asked a lonely cyclist.

'Wantin' petrol?' said the cyclist.

‘Car repairs.’

‘Not at this time of night, mate, not on Christmas Eve. Why not ring the AA?’

‘I’m not a member, I’m afraid.’

‘Nothin’ doing, then, mate,’ said the cyclist, and rode off.

Jack stopped there, his breath smoking in the freezing air. The fog was coming up. They should not stay in a car without lights. A careless lorry could smash it to pieces.

He locked his door, and helped Mariya out. She stooped awkwardly, being very tall, and big with child.

A few steps away was a bed and breakfast hotel, its fanlight decorated with paper chains and tinsel.

Jack rang the bell. They stood on the step holding hands for warmth and reassurance.

‘We’d like to stay for the night,’ said Jack.

‘Sorry, love,’ said the cheerful landlady, ‘closed for Christmas Day. You could try next door. ‘

But next door an elderly man with a bow tie eyed them with disdain.

Married?’ he said.

‘Not yet,” Jack said.

‘Typical,’ said the man, and shut the door. The Immigration Officials had at least let them in, however grudgingly.

The next landlady saw that Mariya was black. ‘Advance bookings only.’ She insisted.

And the one after that asked 'Where's your luggage?'

'In the car,' said Jack. 'We're travelers.'

She slammed the door so hard the windows rattled.

The freezing fog ate into their bones and there was a shower of sleet.

They shuffled warily along the icy pavement. One uncurtained window shone out into the darkness. EMERGENCY HOSTEL, it said.

Mr. Rivers, from the office, watched them come to the door. He rose slowly to his feet, smoothed a few strands of thin hair across his bald head, and peered at them through steel-rimmed spectacles. Years of overwork and under-funding had taken their toll on him. Grey jumper, grey trousers, grey outlook on life.

They sat facing his desk. He noted her advanced pregnancy, and Jack's suntan. Voluntary Service worker from Africa, he guessed. Short of money, but not on the poverty line.

'Can we stay here?' said Jack.

'Both of you?' said Mr. Rivers 'And unmarried?'

'We would have been married, said Jack, 'but the Mission Priest was murdered by the rebels. We only just got away ourselves.'

'We don't have medical facilities. When's the baby due?'

'Not for ten days. We only need a room for one night.'

'Maybe so,' said Mr. Rivers, 'but, as you're unmarried, you can't stay together. Rules of the Charity.'

Jack explained to Mariya in her native tongue. She clung closer to him, and whispered in his ear.

'She's not leaving me,' said Jack. 'She couldn't cope on her own.'

'Hang on,' said Mr. Rivers. He picked up a phone and dialled.

'Rivers speaking,' he said. 'I've got a couple here needing accommodation.'

A voice crackled over the line.

He turned to them. 'How long for?'

'just till tomorrow,' said Jack. 'Our friends can collect us then. But not tonight, in this fog.'

The crackling voice grew angrier.

'Yes, I know you only provide long term accommodation,' said Mr. Rivers, 'but there's nowhere else for them to go. They're just passing through. No, they're not local… ~ Oh, very well. That's the best you can do, is it? And a Happy Christmas to you too!'

He put the phone down in disgust.

'You could have a place together at the Wallingford Refuge. Ten miles from here.'

'We'll sleep in the car,' said Jack.

Easier said than done. They found it with one door swinging open, and the side window smashed. The front seats were soaking wet from the sleet, and spangled with broken glass. Their few precious possessions had gone from the boot. Mariya began to cry hopelessly, The wind blew harder and colder.

'Wait a moment,' said Jack, 'there's something going on.'

The fog lifted. At the end of the street they saw cars on both sides of the road, and heard the sound of music.

Jack led Mariya cautiously forward. Sometimes their feet skidded on the icy pavement. They found themselves under the shadow of a huge building. Carols came from it, and stained glass windows glowed warmly in the darkness. As they stood in wonder, a drunk suddenly barged his way between them, making them let go their hands, and step sharply to each side. Mariya slipped on the ice, and tobogganed down a long flight of steps on her back. She lay in a dark recess near the lowest entrance to the Cathedral.

Jack hurried after her.

'Here,' he said, 'I'll help you up.'

'No,' she said. She knew she was about to give birth.

A flickering light approached. An old woman in cracked shoes and torn stockings lit up the scene with a torch of burning newspaper. She wore an old mac tied with a length of rope and a battered bowler hat, and she took in the situation with bleary eyes.

'Mind ye'self,' she said to Jack, pushing him unceremoniously to one side. 'Queenie knows what to do.'

He squatted against the wall, listening helplessly to Mariya's cries of pain.

'There we come, there we come. Nice and easy,' said Queenie, over and over again until he heard the new-born baby cry.

Then it was safe to move her. Queenie turned two large cardboard boxes into a cot.

‘Keep this,’ she said, handing Mariya a blanket as scratchy as wire wool. ‘I’ll git another termorrer.’

Two more tramps shuffled over.

‘Here y’are,’ said Walt. ‘Just bin brewed.’ It was a chipped enamel mug full of hot sweet tea, straight from the billy-can.

‘Ave this as well,’ said Malky, handing her his precious plastic sheet which kept him warm every night of the year.

‘See ?’ said Queenie, thrilled to have been of help. ‘Snug as a bug in a rug.’

Mariya snuggled her child warmly, crooning a native lullaby. The smile on her white teeth spelt happiness in any language. Jack sat beside her, holding her hand.

‘G’night, lady,’ said Walt.

‘All the best for the kid,’ said Malky, returning to their fire.

Above them towered the Cathedral, the music sounding much clearer now.

‘Happy, ain’t cher?’ said Queenie. ‘You’d fink it was Christmas Day.’

So it was, and the great bells rang out to proclaim it.

ROUTE 169

That night, the three youths were waiting when the double-decker bus pulled up at the Cock & Bottle on the Low Marsh estate. Brad Nesbitt had been warned about them. They went straight to the back of the bus, their best strategic position.

'Fares, please,' said Brad, pleasantly.

'Got no money,' sniggered Jacko, with a cheeky sneer. 'Spent up at the pub.'

'Last driver didn't expect us to pay, did he, lads?' said Les, in an indignant whine.

'Knew what was good for him,' said Kenny, the biggest of the three, with the broad stupid forehead of an ox.

'What I know,' said Brad, 'is that you either pay, or get off the bus.'

'Come on, mates,' said Jacko, his knuckles clenched.

They hauled Brad off the bus, knocked him down, kicked him all over and stamped on his head. Then they sauntered away, leaving no evidence behind.

For a long time afterwards Brad lay in an intensive care ward, in a cat's cradle of drips and wires and tubes.

The Bus company promptly suspended the Route 169 Bus route.

Soon afterwards a new driver appeared at the Depot, Harry Pickstock, a wiry little man in his fifties. With his jutting chin and fierce blue eyes, he was clearly not a man to be trifled with. He had been in REME, he said; reached the rank of corporal, though he looked away when he said it. He obviously knew all there was to know about heavy vehicles.

He breezed through all the practical tests. He waltzed the bus gracefully over the Skid Pan. He passed the tilting test first time, to the applause of those present, and then did it again, in reverse. A silence fell.

He knew to a hair's breadth how far it took to halt a bus travelling at maximum speed. He was everything a driver needed to be; almost too good to be true.

Then he volunteered to drive Route 169 at night. Eyebrows were raised. The other drivers asked what sort of flowers he wanted for his funeral.

'Hardy perennials,' retorted Harry, 'just like me.'

He climbed into his cab carrying a knapsack. Everyone assumed it contained his thermos and sandwiches.

When he got to the Cock & Bottle, the three lads were waiting for him.

'Here's a new driver,' said Jacko, with a big grin.

'Deserves a special welcome,' said Les.

'And we know how,' said Kenny.

Back at the Depot the other drivers were chatting.

'Harry's been in the Army,' said one. 'Should be able to look after himself.'

'But here's a funny thing, said another. "I was talking to a mate of mine, was in REME. Asked him if he knew Corporal Harry Pickstock.

'Not a Corporal,' he said, 'he was our Colonel.' and he described him to a T.'

'What's a retired Colonel doing in our outfit, then? Doesn't make sense.'

The three youths boarded the bus. Harry smiled at them, but never said a word.

'Ain't cha going to ask us for our fares?' said Jacko.

'Cos we got no money, see,' said Les.

Harry smiled even more blandly, Surprise is a key military strategy.

'Ah,' he said, 'but you lads qualify for a £5 bonus, as I've got to take a roundabout route. Catch!'

He threw them each a little bag of coins.

'A Mystery Tour, eh, lads?' said Les.

'Sort of,' said Harry, and the bus started off.

The lads sat at the back. The bus turned into a side road, which had speed bumps. Harry accelerated hard. As the bus hit the first bumps, the lads were almost jolted from their seats.

'Whoa!' said Jacko. 'Want me to lose me back teeth?'

At the second bump, the bus half mounted the kerb, throwing the lads to the right. Jacko jumped to his feet, but the next bump threw him back in his seat.

Les launched himself up the gangway to the driver's cab, and hammered on the window.

'Leave it out!' he said.

The bus swerved violently, flinging him to the floor.

'The guy's a loony!' shouted Kenny.,

But Harry had turned off the road onto the Skid Pan, and was accelerating and braking violently. The bus spun round like a tee-to-tum. Harry switched off all the lights. The lads only knew that the bus was spinning, spinning.

Then it stopped.

'Get him quick, before he kills the lot of us,' shouted Jacko. Still in total darkness, they scrambled forward to the driver's compartment. All of a sudden its light came on. Harry was staring straight at them, his appearance hideously altered; he was wearing a gas mask.

He opened a panel swiftly, and a canister fell to the floor beside them with a heavy clang. A cloud of tear-gas burst from it. They wrenched at the Exit door, but it would not open. Then a second canister went off beside them.

'Up the stairs, quick,' shouted Les, coughing and spluttering. They clattered up to the top deck,. and sat in the front seats. The gas, being heavier than air, lay below them in a thick cloud. They opened a small window vent and huddled against it, desperately sucking in the cold night air.

The bus started off again. Soon it was racing down a narrow road, bounded by the steep banks of a cutting. The bus mounted the bank with its near wheels, and tilted at an alarming angle. But still it raced on.

'He'll have us over in a minute,' screamed Les.

'I'm getting off,' shouted Kenny, 'before we all get killed.'

'Stay still,' said Jacko, 'or we'll overbalance.'

The bus left the bank and righted itself, but still it raced on. Ahead was a low and narrow bridge.

'We'll never make it under there,' screamed Les.

`I'm going down the stairs', said Kenny, but he was soon back again. The tear-gas below was too strong.

'Get on the floor, lads,' said Jacko, so they sprawled on the floor. But still the bus raced on. It was even worse for them lying there blindly, waiting for the crash, and unable to see when it was coming.

Down in the cab, Harry carefully gauged the distance between the bus and the bridge, and braced himself then he slammed on the brakes with all his might.

The tyres screamed, the bus shuddered violently, and soon it stopped. There was a silence. The lads raised their heads cautiously from the floor; their faces were level with the brickwork. The bus had stopped six inches short of the bridge.

'Here,' shouted Les, 'take your money back. We've had enough.'

He tossed his bag of coins down the stairs. It broke, and they rolled around the floor.

Harry said nothing. The bus reversed away from the bridge, then took another country road. Soon they were on a large patch of wasteland at the back of beyond, where mist lay heavily. The bus halted, and the Exit door opened. The tear gas started to drift out into the cold night air. The three lads bundled down the stairs as fast as they could, and out into the darkness. But which way were they to go? They turned this way and that, and were hopelessly lost.

Then they saw Harry striding towards them.

The three lads crouched together.

'Now it's our turn,' said Jacko, ''we'll get you, you bastard.'

'Stand still, men, and listen to me!' commanded Colonel Pickstock in a voice and tone which brooked no denial.

'I have here -' he raised his hand – 'the distributor head from the engine. The bus won't start without it, and none of you knows how to put it back. Attack me, and you'll still be here in the morning.'

They knew they were defeated.

'We're going to come to an agreement. I won't turn you over to the police, and you won't report me for your memorable ride. Agreed?'

They agreed.

'We've some unresolved business to sort out. You remember young Brad Nesbitt, the driver you almost kicked to death?'

'We didn't mean no real harm, like,' said Kenny.

'But you caused him real harm. It's not known when he'll be out of hospital.'

'We're sorry about that. We really are,' said Jacko.

'That's a start, then,' said the Colonel. 'Let's go somewhere more comfortable. We've a lot to talk about.'

They were still sitting in an all-night Transport Café when the sun came up. The Colonel explained that, when he was serving in Northern Ireland, his driver was Sgt. Stuart Nesbitt, who died in ambush from a bullet meant for the Colonel. He promised himself that he'd see young Brad Nesbitt got a good start in life. So he did, till that night at the Cock and Bottle. The Colonel vowed that he'd bring the attackers to justice.

Jacko, Les, and Kenny told him what life was like on the Low Marsh Estate. – no jobs, no prospects, and no hope. They envied the Colonel's life of excitement and responsibility.

'Do you now,' said the Colonel, thoughtfully.

A year went by. The Colonel – now Mr. Harry Pickstock again – set up his own transport firm. Brad Nesbitt is still not very strong, but makes an excellent under-manager in the office.

Jacko, Les and Kenny learned to drive, and are becoming very useful employees under Harry's guidance and encouragement.

They worship the ground he treads on.

SPIDER AND THE FLY

Ursula Brinkley sat in the bar of the Wellington Arms, a rundown pub. She hardly touched the glass of vodka and tonic in front of her. Pale bubbles rose listlessly to the surface, and the drink went flat. She had a grey face, shabby grey hair, a shabby grey coat and a shabby battered suitcase. Who knows where women like that end up, the barman thought. Sleeping on the streets in a cardboard box, and then a pauper's grave. But Harry Hampshire certainly took an interest in her, when he entered the bar. He made a beeline for her, and bought her another vodka and tonic. "Flash Harry," as the barman described him, wore a striped bow tie, trousers with creases so sharp you could have shaved with them, and polished toe-caps you could see to shave in. Why's he interested in a woman like that? The barman thought.

She hardly tasted her drink. 'Mus've had enough', she said woozily.

He took her arm, and walked her unsteadily out with him to his car. The barman went to the window, and jotted down the registration number. It was none of his business, strictly speaking, but he knew what can happen to lonely women who go off with strangers.

There was something a little disturbing about that car. There was a faint smell of choloroform, and a highly unusual clinical cleanliness, due to meticulous hoovering, washing and wiping. No clues would survive in a car like that. Harry had no previous convictions. There was nothing to link him with the middle-aged women whose bodies were found dumped on rubbish tips, waste ground, and in dark alleys. They were all sad grey women, with no friends to miss them. They had all been sexually violated, and violently killed. There was often a faint hint of chloroform in their lungs, too.

Harry stopped the car in the drive of his semi-detached house, and led Ursula inside. He did not often bring women there - it was as well to vary his methods. It was a nondescript area. Students leased flats for a year at a time, and tenants of miserable shops left hastily without paying their rent. His house was more than usually smart for the area, with double-glazing on all the windows. Outside double-glazing, you can never hear a scream.

He led her into the sitting room, and shut the door. There were now two living persons inside that room, and only one of them was going to come out alive.

'Make yourself comfortable,' he said, lighting the gas fire against the chilly winter's night, 'while I put the car away. It's not safe to leave it outside. One can't be too careful.'

He backed the car into his garage, and closed the garage doors. When he brought a body from his back door into the rear of the garage, the deed could never be seen. He always had in mind some lonely spot to drive to, and leave a bulky black bin bag behind. Black bin-bags seldom carry finger-prints, but he wore gloves in any event.

'Now, my dear,' - he said cheerfully as he came back into the room.

'Call me Ursula,' she said.

'Ursula. A nice name. So demure. So suitable. I like to think my name's suitable too. Harry. One can feel safe with Harry.'

'How true,' she said with a trusting smile.

'My mother was a Cynthia,' he said. 'Another lovely name. You remind me of her, you know. She's dead now, unfortunately.'

'Sad,' said Ursula. Her lips quivered, and she almost wept. She seemed to have reached the drunk and tearful stage.

'What would you like to drink now?'

'Nothing, thanks, Harry.'

'Oh, but you must. You must. I insist.'

' 'Nother vodka and tonic, then', she said. 'L'ill one, mustn't stay, though. Need somewhere for the night.'

She hugged her little suitcase, as if someone might steal it. 'Not too 'spensive,' she said.

'The Belle Vue Guest-house, that's the ticket,' he said. 'A lot of my friends go there.'

'Is it nice?' Said Ursula.

'No complaints so far!' Said Harry.

'Bit late, though, tonight?'

'Not at all, he said.' 'Finish your drink.'

'Must just spend a penny,' she said.

'Of course, Ursula,' he said, leading the way to the bathroom.

She got up wearily from the comfortable chair, and trailed her way to the bathroom.

Is it going to happen in the bathroom, then? She thought.

The bathroom was tiled. Stains wash easily from tiles.

No. Her drink was a better method. He mixed her a vodka and tonic, and added something else. It was all so pathetically easy. Unconsciousness, sex and the bin-bag. How many victims would that make in total? He had lost count. Plenty, but never enough. The excitement got better every time. The thrill of the enticement, that was good. Having her at his mercy, was better. His power over her, yes! His cleverness in disposing of the body. And the delicious humour of watching the police running round in little circles, yes, yes, yes! They'd never catch him!

Compared with all that, the sex part was relatively unimportant. Still one doesn't waste opportunities, eh?

Inside the bathroom, Ursula locked the door, and straightened up with a briskness which belied her seeming drunkenness. She donned a little pair of net gloves from her handbag, to leave no traces of her prying fingers. She opened the bathroom cupboard carefully so as to make no noise. She looked swiftly over the contents. Aftershave, mouthwash, toothpaste, safety razor. A bottle of aspirins. She tipped some out into her hand, to make sure. Ordinary aspirins. There was nothing untoward in that bathroom. A moment later she flushed the toilet, and replaced her gloves in her handbag. A weary drunken middle-aged Ursula shuffled out again into the sitting-room.

'Cheers,' said Harry, clinking his glass against hers. It did not smell quite right; she had not expected that it would. Turning away from Harry, she seemed to drink heavily from the glass. She swayed on her feet, and put the glass down so clumsily that much of it was spilt. Smiling blearily, she staggered towards Harry.

'You mus' think me so clumsy,' she said. 'But I've had so much… so much… Ought to lie down…'

She slumped down heavily in one of the armchairs, and leant back in it. Harry bent over her, and her arms went clumsily round his neck, pulling him downwards.

'Harry, Harry,' she mumbled. 'Such nice kind eyes…'

All he could see were her green eyes, looking closely into his until they drooped shut. There was no hurry to drag himself free. The fingers of her left hand were still on the nape of his neck, as a guiding-point for her steel hat-pin. He never noticed her withdraw it quietly with her right hand. He was slightly surprised to feel a tiny prick at the back of his neck. But with a determination born of careful thought and study, she drove the long strong hat-pin its full length through his spinal cord.

His body stiffened, and he fell, paralysed. He had no strength to scream. She watched impassively as he twitched on the carpet for a short time, and then died. She left the pin in his neck; that was part of her self-defence scenario. There was not much more to do. She knocked chairs over higgledy-piggledy, sweeping things off the table as if in a struggle. She drank as much vodka as she dared, keeping her fingerprints off the bottle. Whilst her mind was still clear, she brought a meat-knife from the kitchen and jabbed it into the underside of her forearms, simulating the classic defensive wounds which a victim suffers in trying to ward off a knife attack. Finally – this took more determination than anything else – she closed her right hand rightly round the blade, and wrenched it away with her left hand. This simulated the ugly wound of a desperate woman trying to seize an attacker's knife. She let herself bleed freely over the scene of the struggle. Then she dialled 999.

When the police arrived, it was all too obvious what had

happened. Harry Hampshire had met his end at last, at the hands of a poor drunken woman who had luckily got the better of him. They took a statement from Ursula, and called her to give evidence briefly at the inquest. The coroner expressed his sympathy with her harrowing experience, and hoped that one day she would be able to get over it.

She got over it sooner than he might have guessed. She went back south to her cottage in Somerset, and washed all the grey out of her hair. She put behind her all the nights spent waiting in shabby bars for Harry to arrive. The police never contacted her again. Still, in case they did, she had one last precaution to take. From an envelope hidden at the back of a cupboard she took a newspaper cutting - the main headline, in fact.

MAN CLEARED OF LEEDS MURDER, it said, giving details of the trial in which Harry Hampshire was acquitted of the murder of Lorna Templeton, who was Ursula's elder sister. She lit a candle to her dear dead sister, then put it to the piece of paper. It burnt rapidly, and crumbled into ash. She had become the spider, and she had caught the fly.

STING IN THE TAIL

Mrs. Mompson, a heavily-built woman who could fairly be described as a 'stout matron,' stood sternly in the witness box. The angle of her jaw showed that she was not to be trifled with.

'And then this man' ' she glared at the Defendant – 'turned and faced me on the towpath. His mac was open, and in his clenched fist he held – his Abomination!'

'Where was his hand at this stage?' asked Mr. Framlingham, the prosecuting solicitor.

'Below his waist, of course,' she said.

'So you went straight to the police and lodged a complaint?'

'I certainly did,' said Mrs. Mompson.

'Thank you very much,' said Mr. Framlingham, and sat down.

Innocent persons had nothing to fear from Colonel Marsh, the Chairman of the Bench. He was a lean and bronzed man, with a silver moustache. He had a deep experience of life, and a knowledge of the law which his years on the Bench had taught him. If he formed an immediately unfavourable impression of the Defendant in court, he never gave the slightest indication of it. Nor would he allow that first impression to warp his careful analysis of the evidence.

'Have you any questions you wish to ask the witness?' he said.

'Oh yes,' lisped Wheevil, the Defendant, with a wan smile on his sallow face. There was something so clammy about him, with his thin slicked down hair and his limp hands, that he should have left damp patches wherever he went. He did not so much stand up as oozed himself into a vertical position.

'You've never seen me before, have you?' he said.

'Nor ever want to again,' said Mrs. Mompson.

'When you saw me on the towpath, you were twice as far from me as you are now.'

'But I know what I saw,' she insisted. ''You can't weasel your way out of it like that.'

'Oh, but I CAN,' smirked Wheevil.. 'Let me introduce you to Cuthbert. Perhaps he may refresh your memory.'

He reached into his trouser pocket, and produced something which wriggled in his clenched fist. It was a snake, about five inches long. It was striped blue and red, and its little black tongue darted in and out.

Mrs. Mompson shank back in terror, and even Colonel Marsh stiffened. He had seen active service in India, and snakes.

'Is that a venomous species?' he demanded.

'Oh no,' said Wheevil. 'It is a Red Garter snake. It is as harmless as a grass snake. I doubt if it could even bite. But you wouldn't bite me, would you, Cuthbert?'

Cuthbert flickered his tongue between his lips again.

‘Time for bye-byes now, Cuthbert,’ said Wheevil, putting him back in his pocket.

He turned again towards the witness.

‘Are you sure it wasn’t Cuthbert you saw?’ he asked.

‘Rubbish,’ said Mrs. Mompson, and stormed out of the witness box.

If the prosecution evidence had stopped there, Wheevil would certainly have been convicted. But there was another prosecution witness to come.

‘I call Police Constable Garstang,’ said Mr. Framlingham.

He took the oath, a young officer, fresh-faced and conscientious., who always performed his duty cheerfully, promptly and fearlessly. He had a great career ahead of him.

‘At 2.30 p.m.. on January 4th, acting upon information received,’ sad P.C. Garstang. ‘I proceeded to the Midland Canal, where I saw a man upon the towpath who fitted the description given to me by the last witness. I approached him –’

‘There’s no dispute about these facts,’ said Wheevil from the dock. ‘Just tell the magistrates what I did, and what I said.’

‘Yes, your worships,; said P. C. Garstang, referring to his notebook. ‘I told the accused that a certain complaint had been made to me. He replied, ‘Don’t blame me, blame Cuthbert. I was holding him in my hand at the time.’

‘I asked him where this Cuthbert was, and he said, ‘In my right trouser pocket.’ I told him that I was not satisfied with his explanation, and inserted my hand into the said trouser pocket. Whereupon I was bitten by a certain reptile not currently before the court.’

‘Badly bitten?’

‘No, your worship. I was wearing gloves.’

‘I have no questions, sir,’ said Wheevil. ‘But I would like to give evidence on my own behalf.’

‘So you shall, at two o’clock,’ said Colonel Marsh. “`Meanwhile, the court will rise for lunch.’

In the police canteen, P.C. Garstang was demolishing a large steak and kidney pie when Sgt. Todhunter approached him.

‘A snake in his pocket?’ he said. ‘I heard about another case like that down Ipswich way. And wasn’t there one in Sheffield?’

He made extensive inquiries. There had been seventeen cases up and down the country of a man on a towpath displaying something to middle-aged women. In each case a snake was the explanation, and in each case Mr. Wheevil had been acquitted.

Sgt. Todhunter printed out the full details, and P.C. Garstang raced down to the court with it, and thrust it into Mr. Framlingham’s hand.

‘You’re too late,’ said Mr. Framlingha , ‘Mr. Wheevil certainly travels round the country showing something to women on towpaths, but it might be the snake. It’s not an offence to possess a snake, even with suggestive possibilities.’

‘But if only we’d known earlier, sir! The beaks might have disbelieved him completely.’

‘Can’t be helped,’ said Mr. Framlingham, ‘Mr. Wheevil has never been convicted of anything before, so he is entitled to describe himself as a man of good character. Full marks to your Sergeant, though, for coming up with the other cases.’

Inside their room, the three magistrates considered the evidence.

'She was a very good witness,' said the first.

'On the other hand,' said the second, 'The Defendant gave his explanation to the officer immediately. It isn't something he's thought up since.'

'We all know how careful we must be about mistaken identity,' said Colonel Marsh.

The magistrates resumed their places on the bench.

'We find the case not proved,' said Colonel Marsh.

Wheevil left the dock, grinning broadly. Outside in the corridor, he blocked Mrs. Mompson's route to the door.

'Anyone can make a mistake, love,' he said. 'No hard feelings, eh?'

She swept from the building in a fury, outraged that nobody had believed her.

Wheevil languidly lit a cigarette, and blew a perfect smoke ring. Life had never been better. Once again he had made a fool of a stupid bossy woman – how good that felt! His mother had bossed him, schoolmistresses had bossed him, and aunts had bossed him. Now, in middle age, he was taking his revenge upon bossy women. Once again he had felt the heady buzz of excitement, for each of his appearances in court risked a term of imprisonment. And once again his own cleverness had outsmarted the entire legal system.

Inside the court, Mr. Framlingha rose to his feet again.

'By a curious coincidence, your worships,' he said, 'the next case is also about an unusual pet. The Defendant, Mrs. Rayburn, is an old lady. I appear on behalf of the RSPCA who are absolutely satisfied that she meant no harm. I am instructed that she had a small pet mongoose, and unfortunately had neglected it. It was found in a seriously emaciated condition. I t was kept in a small cage. Perhaps it was too large a bird for its cage.'

'No, Mr. Framlingham,' said Colonel Marsh. 'a mongoose is a small ferret-like animal. It kills snakes.'

"I beg your worship's pardon,' said Mr. Framlingham.

A police officer passed him a message.

"I am told that the animal is here as an exhibit,' said Mr. Framlingham.

'`I would certainly like to see it,' said Colonel Marsh.

The magistrates' clerk was cautiously handing it up to him in its cage, but unfortunately dropped it.

As the cage hit the floor the door sprang open, and the mongoose was thrown out. For a moment of two it lay stunned. Then it lifted its muzzle, and sniffed the air. Its whiskers began to twitch. It caught the scent of an old familiar enemy, and streaked out of court in pursuit, its claws scrabbling and skidding on the stone floor of the entrance hall.

Wheevil blew a last perfect smoke ring. It was time to go home. He and Cuthbert ruled the world! He took Cuthbert out of his pocket, and stroked his head. Cuthbert flickered his tongue again, and his eyes half closed in what seemed to be a moment of sheer pleasure.

'Good old Cuthbert!' said Wheevil tenderly, and put him gently back into his trousers pocket. He never saw that something small, furry and grey was hurtling across the floor towards him. But he certainly noticed it when the mongoose ran up inside the leg of his trousers. There was a deep growl, a sharp hiss, and a flurry of movement inside the garment.

A moment later he was bent double with a scream of agony. Nobody can say whether it was Cuthbert or the mongoose – or, for that matter, both – which caused him a nasty injury. But in any event, and not a minute too soon, justice had been done to `Mr. Wheevil.

THE DIE HARD

Clive Boscombe put down his pint of beer.

"When I was on the St. Nazaire raid - " he said.

All the regulars at the Rat & Rabbit groaned; even Jack Kent, who was Clive's closest friend. He was the only one who was allowed to see Clive's face without a mask, the face which had been so horribly burned when Clive dashed through curtains of blazing petrol to drag one of his wounded mates to safety. Even after cosmetic surgery, which was in its infancy then, it was the face of a Monster from Hell. One eye was always wide open and glaring, a mouth savagely twisted, and cheeks as rough and blazing red as furnace coals.

Clive accepted his own appearance, and, whenever outside his home, always wore a face mask which gave him a bland and pleasant expression.

At the Rat & Rabbit they were all proud of Clive's heroism – he was awarded the Military Cross – but they had heard his story too often.

Yet Clive was always compelled to tell it. He felt guilty because he was one of the few Commandos to escape alive; dozens of them died. Few people nowadays know how daring that raid was, when a British destroyer crammed with explosives rammed its way into French docks vital to the German war effort. It crippled the striking power of the German navy, and showed the world that this target, though seemingly impregnable, was not beyond the range of British daring and determination. Some sixty years had gone by since then, but they weighed lightly on Clive. Even in old age, he still kept himself ready for the next challenge. He jogged for five miles every morning, did press-ups and worked with weights. His thinning hair was now iron-grey; iron was the metal of which he seemed to have been forged.

"We had just landed on the docks," he continued, "when – guess what happened?"

He paused dramatically.

"All hell was let loose," said everybody in chorus.

Clive looked a little crest-fallen. "Did I tell you this story before?"

"Once or twice," said Jack tactfully, "but it's a good story. Tell us again."

So he did, and felt pleasure in it. What else had he to live for? His wife had died many years ago. They had no children - never could have, after some of the injuries he sustained in the St. Nazaire raid.

Clive finished his story – they all dutifully applauded - and soon it was closing time.

"See you next week," they said to each other.

Some shuffled away like the old men they were. Jack walked jauntily with a stick. But Clive marched vigorously back to his little bungalow. He took off his face-mask and placed it in a drawer. He checked that his military cups, trophies and medals were in their proper place in a little cabinet. The medals were for valour, and the campaigns he had served. The cups and trophies were for his success as an Army boxing champion.

Then he undressed, and was soon in bed. "Lights out" at eleven o'clock sharp had always been his habit since his Army days, even without a bugler to play the "Last Post" call. He slept soundly and easily.

At three o'clock in the morning he was awakened by the faint chink of metal against metal. He guessed at once that his flat was being burgled. He sat up in bed and heard whispers, which meant there must be at least two burglars. He got out of bed without making any noise - a skill he had learnt on special missions in the Army. He moved silently to the bedroom door and opened it slightly. The hinges made no noise; he always kept them well oiled. It was part of his regular routine.

He peered into the sitting-room. Two teenage intruders stood there, each holding a torch. He moved back into the shadows, smoothing his chin thoughtfully, and planning his campaign. It was two against one, but he was fighting fit, and had the advantage of surprise. They might be carrying weapons, but that did not bother him; apart from being a boxing champion, he had been trained in unarmed combat, and had faced many different weapons. He felt he was a match for them. Besides, nobody was going to steal his precious military trophies without a battle. From the shadows, he studied the two young men.

"Puffing Billy" Ramsden, as he was known at school, was short, fat and red-faced. His main activity was to sit down playing computer games, a big bag of toffees within reach. He did not want to go burgling, but they had just brought out another expensive computer game which he simply had to have. Whereas Vin Skellitt, his partner in crime, loved burglary for its excitements and profit. He was a senior partner, that is, because he had much more experience - was tall and thin, with a face like a ferret, and with a twisted mouth which showed off his jagged yellow teeth. They were examining their spoils, and looking into the bag which now contained them.

"What d'you reckon?" said Billy, glancing at them briefly.

"Load of crap," said Vin, "cheap tat prizes for winning the Egg and Spoon race, I'd say."

Clive bit his lip furiously, but contained his anger. Icy calm is a great asset in battle, as he knew only too well, but what did they know? Ignorant oiks. He retrieved the icy calm he had learnt so many years ago.

"Let's look in here, then," said Vin, moving towards the bookcase.

Clive was not a great reader – never had been – but he had acquired a lot of books about World War II, and loved to thumb through them and savour the illustrations to carry him back to his world of heroism and nostalgia, especially when anniversaries came round – the outbreak of World War II, the St. Nazaire raid, and VE Day.

"He's got to keep his money somewhere," said Vin, looking around the sparsely furnished room for a hiding-place. "How about here?"

He went to the bookcase, and swept all the books onto the floor. It made Clive grit his teeth, but he maintained his iron self-control. The shelves were now completely empty.

Vin was beside himself with rage. "It's got to be somewhere," he said. "Got to be."

"Saw a film once where the Secret Code was inside the book, in the binding," said Billy.

"Good thinking, mate," said Vin, and seized Vol. I of a handsome set of books, World War II in Pictures. It was one of Clive's favourites.

Vin ripped all the pages out and hurled them across the room. They fluttered to the floor. The book seemed beyond repair.

Billy laughed so much that he never noticed Clive step out of the shadows behind him, and clamp his right hand round Billy's mouth and nose. This was how he had tackled a German sentry at St. Nazaire, silencing him first, and then snapping his neck.

But he only needed to render Billy unconscious. He applied his finger and thumb to certain pressure points at the back of his neck, and Billy slumped to the floor. He would recover soon enough.

Clive switched off Billy's torch. A faint light from the street filtered through the curtains. Vin was on the far side of the room, searching a cupboard by the light of his torch.

"No luck so far," he said.

Billy made no reply.

"No luck, I said," repeated Vin. But when Billy failed to reply a second time, Vin swung round.

Clive was close to him now, and struck out hard with his left hand. The torch went spinning through the air, crashed against the far wall, and fell to the floor with a tinkle of glass.

"Oh!" sneered Vin, taking in the situation at a glance, "I've got company, have I?"

They faced each other one to one, in the almost total darkness of the room., Vin was unarmed. Vin's hands hung loosely at his sides. He moved slowly towards Clive, and circled round him. Clive reckoned he was Vin's equal in this situation.

His fists were clenched, ready to hit out hard. He could have felled Vin with a single blow. But he was born in an age before kick-boxing, and was taken by complete surprise when Vin suddenly kicked him in the pit of his stomach. He fell to the ground, dizzy and winded. Vin stood over him, ready to kick him once more.

Clive was completely defenceless, and Vin knew he was standing over an elderly unarmed man.

"That's you finished, old man!" he sneered.. "Let's see what sort of an old fool you really are."

He laughed, and switched on the light. No-one outside the room could have looked in; the curtains were drawn. But this was his mistake. He found he was looking into the face of the Monster from Hell, a face distorted with anger, the teeth bared, the eyes blazing. He had never seen anything so horrible in his life, not even in the horror videos he loved to watch. But this was real. He staggered back and fell over an armchair. Clive sprang to his feet and pounced on him, turned him face downwards on the carpet, and with a towel lashed his hands together behind his back.

The police came soon afterwards, in answer to Clive's call. Billy and Vin were arrested, and were later sentenced at the Crown Court to twelve months' detention.

Clive always hoped that they would reform and become active and useful citizens. He had often known it happen to raw recruits who had been under his command in the Army. Habits of self-discipline stood everybody in good stead.

After this incident, Clive gathered up all the torn pages of Volume One, and was able to cobble them together again. He could still read and enjoy them. There is also something new now at the Rat & Rabbit. Time after time, Clive puts down his beer glass and launches into a story.

"The night I was burgled," he begins.

THE GHOST BRIDE

Craig Brockbank leant over the rail of the cruise ship Golden Lotus, as it sailed downstream through one of the most spectacular gorges in China, and spat into the mighty river.

'That's not very nice, is it,' said his sister Katya. Her narrow wedge-shaped head and sharp face could almost have been used to split logs. Craig, on the other hand, was massively built; his solid head and brick-red face could almost have driven piles into heavy clay

Sharp and blunt, the two of them were, with an infinite capacity for quarrelling.

'I'm fed up with this trip,' he said.

'It was your idea,' she retorted. 'On a Caribbean cruise we could just have taken it easy all day, with cocktails at sunset. Or if we'd done the Med., we could have visited lots of famous cities. But Oh No, you said, it'll cost us money, you said. But if we made this China trip a so-called fact-finding mission for expanding exports, we could chalk it up against income tax, you said.'

'And what's wrong with that?' he said. "The Chinese might go overboard for Brockbank's Pale Ale.'

'I might go overboard first,' said Katya, sharply. 'You insisted on us sharing a twin-bedded cabin. Cheaper that way, you said. So every might, when you've had a skinful of Chinese bottled beer —'

'I'm only doing Consumer Research on the local produce,' insisted Craig.

'You keep me awake with your snoring. I should be used to you by now, and I've seen you in and out of the bath ever since you were born. It put me off marriage for life.'

'Any would-be husband of yours.' said Craig,' had a lucky escape.'

'I'd have escaped long since,' said Katya, 'if I didn't own half of Brockbank's Brewery. I wouldn't dare leave you to your own devices for this trip. You'd only do something utterly stupid and disastrous.'

A silence followed.

'A lovely day, is it not:' said a voice from benind them. It was dapper Mr. Feng, their Tour Leader, immaculate in the grey linen suit he wore on hot days. He smiled at them from behind a pair of steel-rimmed spectacles, and was a born diplomat.

'Most surely,' said Katya, all smiles too. She knew how to turn on the charm. But Craig remained sour.

'I'd sooner have a London fog, 'he said. 'When are we going to see the read China, anyway?'

Mr. Feng was somewhat surprised.

'I spent several years at our London Trade Centre,' he said. 'Which is the 'real' England? The Tower of London? The Lake District? Spaghetti Junction during the Rush Hour?'

'Not just picture-postcard landscapes and tourist trap museums. anyway,' said Craig. As for the Terracotta Army, when you've seen twenty of those dinky little mascots, you've seen them all."

'But at least you have seen them,' said Mr. Feng, 'They are unique in world history.'

'A toy retinue of soldiers, servants and dancing-girls for the Emperor's life after death?' said Craig. 'It may have seemed a good idea in the Year Dot, but nobody believes in that crap nowadays.'

'Indeed they do,' said Mr. Feng, 'and in this province, too.'

'Really?' said Katya, her interest awakened.

'Most certainly,' said Mr. Feng. 'Many people, who work the land in this region, still believe in it. They are poor and little educated, and still keep up the tradition of the Ghost Bride.'

'A likely story!' said Craig, and turned away. But Katya took Mr. Feng by the sleeve.

'Tell me more,' she said.

'When a bachelor dies,' said Mr. Feng, 'the family want him to have a bride to share his life in the next world. So, when he is buried, he is married to the dead body of an unmarried woman. She is buried with him, and is the Ghost Bride.'

'Where would she come from?' asked Katya.

'From the same village, sometimes,' said Mr. Feng. 'But the families may have to look much further afield. Some will even pay large sums to criminals to have a woman murdered.'

'THAT's the China I'd like to see,' said Craig firmly.

Mr. Feng arranged the whole thing himself. Once the river cruise was over, and the passengers had dispersed, he had a few days to himself. He hired a Land Rover, and the three of them set out into the mountains, stopping the night at a simple inn.

'My old friend Mr. Chang will take good care of you,' said Mr. Feng. 'This part of China is our Wild West.'

Mr. Chang was short and fat, and his big smiling face was round too. You could have rolled him in and out of his inn.

'Welcome, Mr. and Mrs. Blockbank,' he said in broken English.

'We're not married,' said Craig.

Mr. Chang bowed at the correction.

'We're just good friends, as you might say,' said Katya tartly.

Mr. Chang bowed again.

They soon sat down to dinner. The food was delicious. At least, Mr.. Feng thought so. He relished the muttor soup, breaking his bread into it, and the chicken with noodles met his approval also.

Craig swallowed it with ill grace, and his comments on the pickled garlic cloves were unprintable.

After dinner, Craig and Katya went up to their room. It had only one bed, so Katya slept on the floor on a straw mattress. She preferred it that way. It gave Craig less to complain about.

After breakfast, when they left the inn, Craig insisted on driving the Land Rover.

'It's my turn,' he said, 'and I've got a valid licence.'

‘Couldn’t we go a bit slower?’ begged Katya, who was being bounced about on the rough roads.

‘I know what I’m doing,’ said Craig, ‘don’t I, Mr. Feng?’

Mr. Feng maintained a tactful silence. Protests would only have made Craig worse.

For the most part they drove in the baking July heat, but a brief shower of rain made the hard clay tracks slippery and treacherous. Craig took no notice.

His luck ran out as they approached a small village. They came upon a peasant girl driving her geese. A loud blare on the horn made the geese scatter into the air, but the girl froze in alarm. Craig slammed on the brakes, but the tyres skidded. The vehicle threw her onto her back, and the slithering wheels ran over her body. She lay like a rag doll, her dead eyes open in surprise.

‘Now you’ve done it!’ hissed Katya. ‘If they lock you away for a long time it’ll serve you right.’

‘Much better not,’ said Mr. Feng. ‘First of all, we must move the body.’

He and Craig carried her into the back of the vehicle, and covered her over with long grass.

‘I will drop you back at Mr. Chang’s inn,’ said Mr. Feng, ‘ while I make certain arrangements. Do not tell anybody what has happened. Some of the villegers have guns and knives, and are only too ready to use them.’

He returned some hours later. The body had gone.

‘It is all settled and finished,’ he said, and handed Craig a dirty wad of notes.

‘What’s THIS?’ said Katya ominously.

‘For the body,’ said Mr. Feng. ‘`I sold it thirty miles away to a family needing a Ghost Bride for their son. You provided the body, so the money is yours.’

‘I don’t want it,’ said Craig, handing the money back.

‘That’s the first decent thing you’ve done all day,’ said Katya.

‘I will give half the money to the dead girl’s family,’ said Mr. Feng, and put the money in his pocket. ’They are very poor, and will be grateful for that much. And the rest?’

‘Keep it. We’ll return the Land Rover to the hirers,’ said Craig.

‘And I will go my separate ways,’ said Mr. Feng. ‘Goodbye, I do not suppose we shall meet again.’

On the way back to the town, Katya had plenty to say.

‘A fine holiday this has been!’ she said.

‘Shut up!’ said Craig. ‘It’s all over and done with now.’

‘So will we be, if you go on driving like this,’ she snapped

‘I made one mistake, admittedly,’ said Craig, ‘but I’m used to this Land Rover and these roads now. It won’t happen again.’

But it did. He took another corner far too fast, there was a violent skid, and the Land Rover plunged over a cliff. Craig and Katya were killed instantly. Mr. Feng took charge of the situation as soon as he heard of it. He knew from their travel documents that Craig and Katya were each other’s next of kin, so there was nobody in England he could get in touch with. The accident happened after the tour had ended, and was therefore not covered by the usual travel insurance. Besides, bodies had to be buried quickly during the torrid heat of July. He paid Mr. Chang the rest of the money to have them buried locally, with a gravestone to mark their grave, and Mr. Chang followed his instructions faithfully.

That might or might not be the end of the story. Mr. Chang was a kindly man, and could not bear the thought of Craig, whom he knew to be a bachelor, having to face the after-life alone. He assumed that Katya was Craig's mistress – how could it be otherwise, since she shared his room? So, as a special favour and mark of respect, he had a posthumous wedding service performed over them.

If the Ghost Bride superstition is valid – which God forbid – then Craig will remain married for all eternity to his shrew of a sister.

THE GLAD RAGS

Fred stood by the wardrobe.

'Which one do you think, love?' He asked.

'The black one,' said Ruby firmly. 'On a bright day like this, its little failings will hardly show.'

Most of their clothes had some little failings - a bare patch here, a darned hole there. It hardly mattered on Acacia Road, but on special occasions when they donned their "glad rags", they liked to be seen at their best.

The black jacket had a frayed right cuff, through which the white basting showed. Fred used real black ink on it – not biro, which went a sort of shiny mauve when the light caught it. He sewed the edges together with dull black thread.

'Do you think the jacket could do with another brush?' Said Fred.

'If you're careful,' said Ruby.

'Must I always be careful?' Said Fred, putting his arm slyly round her waist.

‘Now, now,’ said Ruby, ‘we’re almost too old for reckless abandon.’

‘Almost,’ said Fred.

Soon they were ready, Ruby in her little black dress, and one of those wide-brimmed hats without which holy matrimony is never properly observed. They stepped out into the sunshine. Fred carried a mac over his arm, carefully folded to hide a faded stain.

Which one did you say it was? Asked Ruby, on their way to the bus stop.

St. Clare’s, said Fred. We did St. Augustine’s last week.

So we did, said Ruby. We don’t want to get too well known.

Fred checked the details copied out of the local paper at the Public Library. That saved having to buy it. There were quite a few weddings that Saturday, but afternoon ones were the best. Morning ones usually meant a reception out of town beyond the bus routes. So St. Clare’s it was.

Bride or groom? Asked the Best Man, at the church.

A bit of both, really, said Fred. It was safer.

Would you mind sitting on the bride’s side, then? Said the Best Man, It evens up the numbers.

Ruby looked doubtfully at Fred. Which was better? On the more crowded side, you passed unnoticed. But on the sparser side, people got talking to you, and you might sneak into the Reception on the strength of it.

The Receptions were the thing. Buffets were the best, you could keep on the move, and move away if awkward questions were asked. Buffets gave you more of a chance of a good tuck-in.

'I could do with a good square meal,' said Fred. 'Our diet has been a bit "rhomboid" recently.'

You could never tell from the Venue. They once got into a Reception at the Clarendon - the Clarendon, I ask you - where the champagne cost a fortune a bottle, but all you got to eat were postage-stamp sandwiches. Tiny little squares of thin sandwiches with the thinnest possible layer of meat or caviar. Whereas at the Red Lion Rooms you got Pork Pies and Beef Salad and Salmon Rolls and Prawn vol-au-vents. And chicken legs! As the guests drifted away, there were still two platefuls all dressed up in little paper frills, and nowhere to go. That was when they invented Rex, their Golden Labrador, as a pretext. They never had a dog – couldn't afford it, hadn't room for it – and it wouldn't have been allowed in Flat 3B anyway. But 6 chicken legs would have lasted over the week-end, if they got them straight into the fridge. A quiet word with the waitress, and the chicken legs in a paper bag were stuffed into the pocket of Fred's mac. Only a paper bag – so grease got out and stained the mac. Ever since then Fred kept the mac carefully folded, though the stain was beginning to fade.

Fred and Ruby sat on the left side of the church, looking like everybody's favourite uncle and aunt, genuine smiles and false teeth.

'I don't think he eats many postage stamps,' whispered Fred.

They looked across the aisle at a bald, red-faced man almost bursting out of his pearl-grey waistcoat. One deep breath, and something would have given.

Fred's tummy started rumbling.

'You should have had those last two potatoes' whispered Ruby.

'I was saving them for tomorrow,' whispered Fred.

A glove fell on the pew in front of them. Fred returned it to the lady with a polished smile.

'Lovely day for the wedding,' he said.

(Always safe as an opening. The next tactic was to form a link.)

'May we introduce ourselves?' He said. 'Fred and Ruby Dymond.'

'I'm Marianne Binns,' said the lady. 'Have you known the Woodchurches long?'

'I think we know the Stewarts better,' said Ruby.

'Stewarts?' Asked Marianne, puzzled.

Ruby hastily glanced at the printed order of service.

'Fenby, I meant,' she said, 'Silly me. We always called him Stewart. He seemed to prefer it.'

'Fancy that,' said Marianne.

'We saw the family sometimes in Lowestoft, ' said Ruby hurriedly. 'Mostly in summer. When we were working.'

'Touring with Max Bygraves,' said Fred. 'In Old-Time Music-Hall.'

'How nice,' said Marianne.

'Oh, it was, it was,' said Ruby.

Which was true. They were once booked in with him for three weeks, when one of the novelty acrobats sprained his wrist. Fred and Ruby's names were almost at the bottom of the bill.

THE DIAMONDS.
Twinkling feet and sparkling comedy.

'Max Bygraves is terribly good, isn't he,' said Marianne.

(Show-business people are always so loyal, especially when basking in reflected glory.)

'He really liked our act,' said Fred. 'He said we were lovely people.'

Just then Mrs. Woodchurch, the Bride's mother, arrived, a stout widow who stood clutching her handbag, as if someone might snatch it. The organ played and everyone turned as the Bride came up the aisle on her uncle's arm.

Marianne turned to Fred and Ruby.

'We always said Coral was the marrying kind,' she whispered. This could hardly be disputed; she was eight months pregnant. Her mother glared fiercely at the congregation, as if they were all accomplices in her daughter's fall from innocence.

Outside the church, wedding photos were taken, and cars moved off to the reception.

'Have you got transport?' Asked Marianne.

'We don't want to put you to any inconvenience,' said Ruby.

'Not at all,' said Marianne, 'it's not far away.'

That was all right, then; they could get home again afterwards by bus, or walk, if they had to.

An elegant sign in copperplate lettering marked The Devereux Rooms, which stood in a shabby side-street off a busy trunk road.

There were more pin-ball machines in the entrance-hall than Mrs. Woodchurch would have liked, but when a wedding is arranged at short notice, one has to take what one can get. Still, a feast is a feast the world over.

As they followed Marianne in through the main door, Fred and Ruby got a view of the kitchen. There were chicken legs and salad on real china plates. Inside the Magnolia Suite, with the barman as Master of Ceremonies, the happy couple and .parents were lined up ready to receive the guests. The fat man in the threatened waistcoat handed in his invitation card.

'Mr. PERCY CHALLINOR,' announced the barman.

Next came Marianne, with her card.

'Mrs. MARIANNE BINNS,' he read aloud.

Fred and Ruby were next in line. The barman put out his hand for their card. Fred and Ruby exchanged glances. They could only be asked to leave.

Fred patted his pockets as if he had just lost his invitation. Mrs. Woodchurch saw him, and her mouth tightened.

'Your name, sir?' Said the barman.

Fred told him.

'Mrs. and Mrs. FREDERICK DYMOND,' he announced. They entered the room, and shook hands with the bridegroom and his parents, who had no reason to question their presence.

When they came to the Bride, Ruby took her hand in her own.

'We just know you're going to be happy, don't we Fred? We just know it.'

The Bride looked pink with pleasure. Mrs. Woodchurch shook hands in silence This was not the moment for a confrontation.

'It's been a lovely wedding, Mrs. Woodchurch,' said Fred. 'It's a privilege to be here.'

As they walked on, they could feel her eyes on their backs like a poised stiletto.

They mingled among the guests.

'You come from Birmingham, do you?' said Ruby to a couple. 'We've worked at Birmingham, haven't we, Fred?'

'With Max Bygraves,' said Fred. 'Perhaps you came and saw us.'

The last few guests were approaching the line-up when Coral clutched her husband's arm and closed her eyes.

'What's the matter, darling?' he asked her.

'It's nothing,' she said. 'Nothing, really.'

The barman rapped on a table with his wooden hammer for attention.

'Ladies and Gentlemen,' he said, 'please make your way into the dining-room. You will find a seating plan by the door, and your names are in your places as well.'

The guests were soon buzzing round the seating-plan. Fred and Ruby found themselves at the back of the queue.

A couple may not have turned up, said Ruby. There were six glasses of wine still untouched on a table; they always looked for omens like that.

'If everybody's here, we'll slope off,' said Fred.

They turned round to see Mrs Woodchurch staring straight at them. She had overheard one of the groom's guests say he thought the place was a bit common, and she was looking for a victim. She moved rapidly.

'I thought you weren't invited, and you're not,' she said. 'Perhaps you would care to explain.'

She did not want an explanation, only a chance to work herself into a fury. Moments like this were always to be savoured.

'We meant no harm,' said Fred, but the Best Man took Mrs. Woodchurch's arm and whispered something in her ear.

'I think something's starting to happen,' he said.

Mrs. Woodchurch turned around. Her daughter was leaning back in a chair, her hand on her stomach.

'What are we going to do?' Asked Mrs. Woodchurch.

'Let me have a look at her,' said Ruby. 'I was trained as a nurse.'

Mrs. Woodchurch nodded gratefully.

A moment later she was at Coral's side, speaking to her gently.

'Let's find somewhere quiet for a minute,' said Ruby. She steered Coral out of the Magnolia Suite into the Orchid Room, which was not in use

Fred started to follow them.

'Girls only,' said Ruby firmly, closing the door in his face.

The Best Man hurried back into the dining-room. 'I've rung the doctor,' he said, 'he'll be here in ten minutes.'

'We can't start the meal without Coral,' said Mrs. Woodchurch.

'Let me handle this,' said Fred. He moved to the top table, and picked up the microphone.

'Ladies and Gentlemen,' he said, 'Is this mike live?'

He tapped it.

'Yes, it is. I could tap my own head in the same way, but it doesn't make a noise. At least, I hope not.'

There was laughter.

'This afternoon you have a special surprise,' he said, 'by courtesy of our gracious hostess, Mrs. Woodchurch,'

He turned towards her, smiling and clapping, and the audience followed suit.

'We are going to start with a a little entertainment. You didn't know that, did you? That's the surprise. And here to entertain you is Yours Truly, and my dearly beloved Ruby, who will be with us very shortly. Fred and Ruby Dymond. We may not be famous, but I hope we're fun.'

He was now well into his stage routine.

'So this afternoon it's fun first, and food afterwards. Five minutes ago I heard someone say, I could eat a horse. I could eat a horse. Well, I'm sorry to disappoint you, but horses aren't on the menu tonight. They're not easy to get hold of at full gallop.' (There was laughter). 'They're not easy to get hold lf at a canter, and the less I say about the trots, the better.' (More laughter).

'Sardines aren't easy to get hold of, either. It's the oil that makes them so slippery.' (Laughter).

The doctor put away his stethoscope. 'It's a false alarm, he said, but if your daughter has any urgent problems - take her straight to the maternity hospital. And if – '

He looked at Ruby.

'I'll go with her,' said Ruby. 'Glad to.'

'Thanks ever so, Ruby,' said Coral.

'You're very kind,' said Mrs. Woodchurch, and kissed her. The doctor departed.

In the dining-room, Fred was singing at the piano. The audience was eating out of his hand.

'She is my Lily of Laguna, she is my lily, and my beau. Come on everybody, join in the chorus.'

Which they did.

'She's my lady-love –

'That's it,' said Fred. 'Let's be hearing you.'

In the middle of the chorus, Ruby took over at the piano, and Fred did a tap-dance. There was a burst of applause.

Fred and Ruby sat at the top table.

'Coral, or should I say Mrs. Fenby – I want her to get used to the idea,' said the groom. (Laughter) 'We are both grateful to you two for coming to support us.

I am also grateful to Mrs. Woodchurch for her splendid hospitality, but especially for being such a lovely person.' (Applause. Mrs. Woodchurch looked positively radiant). 'If it wasn't for her, we wouldn't be here. If it wasn't for her, Coral wouldn't be here either.' (More laughter and applause). 'Finally I'd like to say a special word of thanks to Fred and Ruby helping make this such a special occasion. While the chef was catching the sardines.‘ (Laughter. Fred and Ruby stood and bowed.)

The wedding cake was cut, and the guests dispersed. Mrs. Woodchurch tossed her head before a tear could run down her cheek.

Marianne stopped her car beside Fred and Ruby.

‘Would you like a lift home?‘ She said.

‘No, thank you very much,‘ they said.

The buses were still running, and they did not want her to see Acacia Road. But Mrs. Woodchurch stopped them next. ‘I hope you won’t mind my saying this, but my daughter’s married an accountant. It’s not really my scene. I’ll be on my own now. But if you ever fancy a bottle of ale – ‘

‘Brown ale,‘ said Ruby. ‘After a Welsh Rarebit.‘

They hugged each other, and Ruby called her Gladys.

Back in their room Ruby took off her Glad Rags.

‘I’m a teeny bit squiffy,‘ she said.

‘This shoulder seam,‘ said Fred, ‘is giving way. It was all that dancing.‘

‘It’ll last a big longer if you treat it gently,‘ said Ruby. ‘Lots of things will.‘ .

She put her arms round his neck.

THE LONE WOLF

Shaun Sullivan sat at an outside table at the Café Des Bons Amis, not far from the Faubourg St. Germain. Watching people go by, especially pretty girls, was all he usually did. He sat there with a single cup of coffee, which was all he usually drank. He hoped a generous-minded friend would stop by, though it seldom happened. He could not be described as a drifter, because drifters tend to move from one place to another. At the age of 44, he had ceased to take any active steps to further his lifestyle. He had given up trying to find a steady job, and described himself proudly as "independent." He regarded life as having treated him unfairly. He used to tell people that he had been unlucky of late. But luck had nothing to do with it. He had a perfect genius for picking the slowest horses running at Longchamps.

So he sat at his usual table in the one shabby suit he always wore. His face could not be described as vacuous, because it showed the occasional spark of intelligence. He was clean shaven or otherwise depending on which he first found when he got up of a morning – his razor or a bottle. If the bottle won, his shave would be adjourned until the following day, as was the present case.

At the table next to him, a business man in his fifties sat impatiently, drumming his fingers on the table. He wore a sharp suit and tie, and had a well-trimmed beard, manicured nails, and an elegant briefcase which showed no signs of wear.

He took no notice of Sean Sullivan, who was not his style at all. But Shaun swivelled his gaze to take him in, because – who knows – he might offer him a job or at least an errand which could earn him a few coins. Then Sean noticed a heavily-built woman who was standing a little to one side of the café. Glamour and elegance played no part in her life. She was looking from side to side furtively before she strode across to the businessman.

"Ludmilla," she said in a strong Russian accent. He nodded, and she sat down. She had something urgent to say, and was in a hurry to say it. She groped in her handbag for some papers, and laid them swiftly before him. He scooped them up hastily into his briefcase, and they left the café in opposite directions. As they left, a piece of paper fluttered to the ground. Shaun picked it up, and called after them, but they did not hear him. It was a page from a notebook, and written on it was the day's date plus 39 Avenue Clichy, 10:30 p.m. And the meaningless words 79 XJW.

It demanded his attention, because he had nothing else to do. So Sean went there that night to return their piece of paper. It was none of his business, of course, but they might have given him something for his trouble. The house was in darkness. Shaun tried to peer through the front window, but all the curtains were drawn. So he rang the bell. Twice, and nobody answered. Then he noticed that the front door was slightly ajar. He pushed it open, and turned on the lights in the hall.

'Is anybody there?' he shouted.

Once, twice and three times.

Nobody answered, least of all the bearded businessman from the café. He was lying on his back on the hall floor, a silver paper-knife through his heart. On a piece of paper, clutched in his hand, were written the words 'Moliere. The Flowers of Evil.'

All of a sudden of the lights went out. Shaun heard a scuttling upstairs, like a rat in an attic, and someone clattered down the stairs and out through the front door, which was slammed.

Then silence. The hairs on the back of Sean's neck stood up, and he too bolted out of the house. He came home as fast as he could, and studied the note.

What did it mean? Something to do with Moliere, obviously.

But Moliere did not write The Flowers of Evil, a famous book of poems. Every French schoolchild knows that. Baudelaire did. What were The Flowers of Evil, in this case? It might mean the proceeds of a robbery, or a drug deal. Or the Russian Revolution, thought Shaun. Moliere might be a clue. He was born in Paris, but nobody knows exactly where. Moliere had one fixed address, at least; his burial place, the famous Pere Lachaise cemetery, a place of special honour, rather like being buried in Westminster Abbey.

When Shaun left the house 39 Avenue Clichy, he did not bother to look into the shadows, and would probably not have spotted the thin man who almost melted into the brickwork. He was short and wiry, dressed all in grey, and had a cadaverous face with eyes so sunken they almost disappeared. He followed Shaun at a safe distance, on soundless rubber-soled shoes, till Shaun entered the cheap hotel where he lived. Shaun ran up the stairs two at a time, and let himself into his upstairs room – it came cheapest – flung himself down onto his unmade bed, and was soon fast asleep. The thin man never shifted his position outside.

When Shaun woke up, it was broad daylight. He gulped down a cup of coffee, and made his way hurriedly to Moliere's tomb. It stood on four columns; behind one of them, hard to see, was taped a small brown envelope. . Inside it was a little key and a ticket for a railway station left-luggage locker. He tried the Gare du Nord, and was lucky first time. He opened locker 79 and found a small metal suitcase with a combination lock. He hurried home to open it. The thin man followed him. Then, using the letters XJW, Shaun opened the case. Inside was a big envelope written in old-fashioned handwriting, with an old postcard of Moscow in it and a thick wad of Russian currency, with a face-value of millions of rubles. How Shaun laughed! He was on easy street now! He went to a bank.

"I want to make a deposit," he said to the bank clerk.

"Monsieur has an account?" said the clerk.

"Not yet," said Shaun. "But I'll open one right now. I've got loads of money here."

He laid the wad of roubles on the counter.

"It is not as easy as that," said the clerk. "We only take money from strangers very carefully. In case the money comes from crime."

The Flowers of Evil, Shaun thought.

"But this money we cannot take in any event," continued the clerk.

"Why not?" said Shaun. "Don't you accept Russian money?"

"Of course," said the clerk. "But this is Imperial Russian money. It hasn't been valid since the Revolution."

"It has no value at all?"

"Monsieur Painlevé, our foreign expert, will tell you."

He came forward, and looked lovingly at the money.

They carried pictures of Peter the Great, and a well-built woman who represented Mother Russia.

"Beautiful," he said, "really beautiful. I have never seen the old currency in such mint condition. But it has little value save as antiques."

He returned the money. Shaun put it back in the envelope, and departed.

Back in his room he picked up one crisp and elegant banknote. How much, he wondered, had it been worth to its owner, who perhaps had money to burn. Shaun was in the same position, and lit a candle. He held the banknote into the flame. It burned slowly, whilst the Russian figures danced, turned black and crumbled. Then he put a whole handful of notes into the empty grate, lit them, and watched them burn to ashes. He tossed the envelope onto them too.

A violent blow on the door made him jump. Shaun went to the door, and opened it. The thin man stood there, his face as hard as hewn rock.

"Where it is?" he asked, with a heavy Russian accent.

"Where is what?" Shaun said.

He struck Shaun a blow on his chest which sent him staggering backwards.

"The treasure."

"What treasure?"

"From Moliere's tomb. I followed you."

"I never saw you," Shaun said.

"Nobody ever does," said the man. "Now, where it is?"

"Most of the money is still here. I burned some of it."

"Trash," said the man. "But the other item?"

"There wasn't anything else," Shaun said, "apart from a postcard."

"Precisely that," said the thin man, his eyes narrowing. "Where it is?"

"I don't know."

"Did you read it?"

"'Tout est complet,' I think it said. Everything is ready, it means."

The other man's eyes glittered. "I know what it means. But was it signed?"

"Only by initials, if I remember. I didn't take much notice."

'You didn't take much notice!!!' said the other man, as if talking to a stupid child.

"Not really, no."

He pushed up so close to Shaun that he backed against the wall.

"Those initials. Might they have been V - I – L?"

"Now you come to mention it, yes. I wondered at the time if they had anything to do with The Flowers of Evil."

"You do not know who V.I. L was?"

Shaun shook his head.

"Then I tell you."

He gave him the name, underlining every single syllable with his voice.

"Vlad-i-mir Il-yich Ul-a-nov."

Shaun still looked blank.

"That was the original name of Comrade Lenin, before he changed it to escape the Tsarist secret police. That is why he fled to Paris, so as to continue his activities. He was then, so to speak, a Lone Wolf. That is an expression applied to terrorists who have to act on their own. But he wanted to build up his own organisation, without which his activities were doomed to failure. Do you now see the importance of that postcard? It showed him starting to recruit others to work with him. You could say that the message, all is ready, together with the money he had gathered together, marked the beginning of the Russian Revolution. In other words, this is the most important and valuable postcard in the history of the world. And you say you have lost it!"

"No, I threw it away," Shaun remembered, "into the waste paper basket. I didn't think it was worth keeping."

The man pounced on the waste paper basket in the corner of the room, but there was nothing there.

"I emptied it into the dustbin downstairs," Shaun said. "Today is the day they collect the rubbish."

Without a moment's hesitation the thin man tore from the room, and shot down the stairs. Shaun watched from his back window as he ran into the yard, and pulled the lid off the only dustbin that was there. It was empty. He heard the sound of the rubbish collection vehicle further down the road; they had already emptied ten more bins into the back of it.

Shaun saw him dash to it, and climb onto the back. In a desperate attempt to find the postcard, he was throwing all the rubbish back out into the road, until a gendarme arrested him. Then the rubbish vehicle accelerated away round the corner, and was lost to sight.

Shaun preferred not to wait until he came back, so he went to his favourite café. He ordered a coffee, and reflected upon the fact that he had escaped the fate of the other man who had been stabbed to death with a silver paper-knife. Shaun had been unlucky enough to lose the chance of selling that postcard for a vast sum of money, but that was the story of his life. He sipped his coffee, and watched the pretty girls go by.

THE SEAGULL

Una put her suitcase down on the bed, and looked out of the window. On the horizon was the narrow strip of sea which earned the Seaview Private Hotel its name. She opened the window, breathed the sea air in deeply, and breathed it out slowly and evenly. Twelve times.

'What you need is a short break and some good sea air', her doctor had told her. He was right; she felt better already.

She closed the window, and was changing into her demure grey dress when a rapping on the pane startled her. On the window-sill stood a gull with proud imperious eyes.

Una spread the remains of her sandwiches on the sill. The gull devoured them eagerly.

There was a sharp rap at the door. The landlady stood there, all pride and authority.

'Have you read the RULES?' She demanded.

'Not yet,' faltered Una.

'NO animals to be allowed in rooms, and NO birds to be fed. But what do I find?

'I'm sorry, Mrs. Neelson,' said Una.

'The trouble they give us, doing their droppings on my front steps. Who has to clear it up, may I ask?'

'I'm sorry,' said Una again.

'MAY I EMPHASISE,' added Mrs. Neelson, 'NO guests may bring visitors into the hotel without my express permission. Above all, NO men in your room.'

'Of course not,' said Una.

'Dinner is at seven sharp,' said Mrs. Neelson. You have been allotted Table No. 5. Welcome to the Seaview Private Hotel.'

She left the room as if she owned it, which of course she did.

Una gathered up her raincoat, and went out to see the sights of Seahaven, such as they were. She bought a copy of Women's Pictorial, and sat in one of the shelters on the prom. She had time to read it from cover to cover - a real orgy of leisure. She felt a bit chilly, but she would warm up soon with a pot of tea and a toasted tea cake at a nice café. Her doctor was right; it was doing her good.

Dinner at seven sharp. She sat with her library book beside her on the plate. Mrs. Neelson's mouth tightened; she preferred her guests to focus on the food.

Una started with clear soup –ConSOM was what the waitress called it – followed by a breaded plaice fillet and two veg. At the corner table a young mother and two children were chattering away happily. Una smiled at them, and they waved back. She wondered what it would have been like to have children of her own. It was too late now.

She slept soundly that night, and was wakened by the seagull tapping on her window. She ignored it, and went downstairs for the Continental Breakfast. The Full English breakfast was Extra, and there was no point in throwing money about.

Later she took a coach excursion to Staunton Castle and the Paradise Gardens, and took a few snaps with her little camera.

It was a happy day.

That night, at dinner, Una was just eating her bread-and-butter pudding when a man in a blazer sat down at a nearby table. He was quite good-looking, she thought, with a breezy air and ready smile which he shared with everyone, including her. She smiled pleasantly back. That was all.

Next morning, having finished her library book, she bought a Mills & Boon romance from a charity shop. She was just about to leave when a flame-coloured gown caught her eye. It had a plunging neckline - her mother would have had a fit! She took a very deep breath and bought it. And a shade of lipstick to match. And some perfume. And an uplift bra. She had almost exhausted her spare funds, but it seemed worth it.

That night, greatly daring, she wore them all at dinner. Mrs. Neelson was appalled. But Una did not care. She was taking her cue from the seagull, strutting proudly. This was her opportunity, her big extravagance, her big adventure.

The man at the corner table smiled at her.

All dressed up and nowhere to go?' He asked.

'I'm afraid so,' she said.

'There's a dance tonight at the Winter Gardens,' he said. 'Care to come along?'

It was almost a blind date! And not a moment too soon! Her mother would have had another fit. Even when Una was just out of school, and really quite pretty, her mother had shooed her boy friends away.

'I don't think he's quite suitable,' she would say, or 'Too good looking-'

By such stratagems she kept Una at home till she herself became an invalid, and Una's beauty had faded beyond hopes of romance. She had given her invalid mother the best years of her life, but now it was time to kick over the traces. What had she to lose? She doubted that Clive – that was his name – would take advantage of her. It was time for an adventure. The seagull told her so.

Clive was rather a good dancer, and she didn't do badly herself. During the interval she asked what he did for a living.

He travelled in patent medicines, he said, including PainFree, a much advertised aspirin.

'Oh, I take that myself,' she cried, glad to find a common bond. 'What else do you sell?'

'You wouldn't want to know,' he said firmly.

'Go on,' she sad skittishly, 'I'm a grown woman.'

'Promise me you won't laugh?'

'Promise.'

'It's an ointment,' he said, and then whispered, 'For something rather embarrassing.'

She had to cram her hanky into her mouth to stop herself laughing.

'I don't take anything like that,' she said.

'I know,' said Clive, 'I can tell, by the way you sit.'

'Is there anything else you can tell from the way I sit?' She asked roguishly.

'Need I ask?,' said Clive, meaningfully.

She blushed to the roots of her hair. That did it. That broke the ice. Suddenly, in that interval at the Winter Gardens, they poured out their hearts to each other.

She had been rather a good pianist, and would have liked to have taken it up professionally. But her mother stopped her.

Clive showed her the photos of his wife and children. He was hardly cheating on her by going to a dance. He confessed his terrible fear that, in middle age, he would be made redundant.

They danced the Last Waltz cheek to cheek, silent and serene. Then they hurried back along empty streets. Mrs. Neelson had an eleven o'clock curfew. A sudden shower of rain drove them into a dark shop doorway. All of a sudden she was in his arms in a passionate kiss, her eyes tight shut. In the distance a clock began to strike. They raced back to the hotel, and met the baleful glare of Mrs Neelson, who handed them their keys in silence.

'It was wonderful,' whispered Una, at the foot of the stairs.

'No harm done, eh?' Said Clive.

Those were their last words together.

Una woke the next morning with the seagull rapping at the window.

Clive had checked out early. She kept back a roll from breakfast to give the seagull, but it had flown away. She packed her bag, paid her bill, and walked to the station. A gentle sun was drying the wet pavements.

THE STREET-WALKER

She walked the streets, not knowing where to go or what to do. Margaret Kemplin, known to everyone as Molly, could be described as on the run, except that she was not running, but limping. She had tramped miles and miles since she left the Holly Road Remand Centre, and she had no wish to go back to it. The other girls bullied her unmercifully there, not only because she was the smallest and weakest - criminals always like to bully - but because her crimes were such small beer as to be almost beneath contempt. What had she done?

Snatched items of clothing from Mercers, the big stores; secreted bottles of perfume under her clothing from Nash & Unwin, the chemists; and stolen chops of meat from Brumby's the butcher.

Then there were numerous "kiting" offences. "Kiting" means using a stolen pension book to obtain money, by forging the owner's signature.

If she went to the Cat and Cabbage pub., she could pick up a stolen pension book for a fiver and could use it for getting money at different post offices. The trouble was that she was too well known within a five-mile radius of her home, and had to go to post offices as far away as Whitney Green. Yet even here she had little success, because she looked far too young to have a pension book in her own right. That is why she was frequently caught.

The magistrates decided that she needed to be sentenced by the Crown Court, and remanded her in custody to the Holly Road Remand centre. But she broke out of it again and again.

Zena was her chief problem, a strapping girl with big fists and a bigger temper. This was not Molly's worst fear. Zena fancied anyone on two legs, regardless of their sexual track record. If Zena got her in a corner and kissed her, there was no telling what disease she might pass on. She had ugly scabs round her mouth, which boded ill.

Zena fancied Molly because she was young and fresh. So long as she remained in Holly Road, she was on risk of becoming a victim.

So Molly ran away, in the dusk of a November evening, when the rain was falling in a sleety drizzle, and her thin shoes squelched because they were wet through. She knew that her absence would be noticed, and that the police would be anxious to pick her up. All the more reason therefore to keep off the main roads and dodge in and out of dark doorways whenever a car's headlights swept the street. She knew the police would be visiting all her favourite places, so she had to make use of squats, those empty houses where the front door was boarded up, and the windows covered with corrugated iron. There was one in particular where she felt safe; it was 15 Jagger Street, where the only means of entrance was a back window facing the gasworks.

Here she hid that night, sleeping on a mattress green with mould, with no heat or comfort at all apart from a filthy blanket she found lying on the floor.

On the next morning she sneaked out in in search of food. She reached the back entrance to a bakery, where trays of bread were being loaded into vans for delivery to the food shops. She sneaked a large loaf of bread – still lovely and warm from the oven – and pushed it under her sweater. In a disused hovel behind the bus station she took refuge, and crammed all the slices of bread into her mouth, two at a time. Someone had left a bottle of Coca-Cola half empty In a corner she picked it up and drained it gratefully. It was flat and had its fair share of grit, but she drank it is gratefully as if it was a great delicacy.

What was she to do now? The whole day lay before her, with nothing to do but dodge the police. She found herself at the Cooper Street market, which was always crowded at that time of the day. Here she would not attract attention by being on her own. But she could not stay there all day. She edged her way to the entrance, and peered out along Cooper Street. There were no signs of any police officers there. But she did notice Randy Griffin, who was lounging against the wall of the pensions office. He had no business to be there, because he had no pension to draw. But at once she realised what was going to happen. Randy Griffin and his mate Jogger Martin always worked in pairs, ready to rob anybody, or snatch a handbag, or pick a pocket. Jogger Martin was standing 50 yards away at the mouth of an alley, pretending to read a newspaper. At once she realised what their plan must be. As soon as a vulnerable member of the public emerged from the pensions office, having drawn out their week's money, which could well be as much as £100, they would set upon her and be sure of getting the money. Jogger was holding a heavy stick, which he would not hesitate to use.

Two minutes later an elderly woman came out onto the street from the pensions office. She was carrying a white stick, and was feeling her way along the pavement. She was obviously partially sighted, and therefore an ideal victim. As she walked away from the pensions office, Randy Griffin started to follow her. In a moment or two she would find herself sandwiched between the two thugs. Her money would be gone, and she would be lucky to escape serious injury.

Molly was not a regular champion of vulnerable people, and did not give herself readily to good causes. But the thought of these two getting the better of the poor old woman was too much for her. The old lady looked a little like her own grandmother, if the truth be told. That was another reason for spurring her on. Perhaps if she had given the matter much thought, she would not have intervened. The risk might not have been worth it. But a sense of justice prevailed over caution. She hurled herself across the street, and cannoned violently against Jogger Martin. She knocked him off balance; he fell backwards into the alley. The old lady hastily shuffled away. Molly took off her shoe and hit Randy Griffin on the forehead with the heel of it. He was stunned, and sank down on the pavement. But Jogger Martin was on his feet again in a flash, and set about her with his heavy stick. Many were the blows he struck in vengeance for her interference. They caught her on the head and shoulders and arms. She was not a strong girl by any means, and these blows disabled her completely. Her left wrist was broken where she raised her arm to defend herself. But her actions had not been in vain. Members of the public ran across to the old lady, and apprehended the two villains.

The police arrived soon afterwards and took them into custody.

One of the officers was Sgt. Baker, who had been looking for Molly.

'So there you are!' he said, helping her into a separate police car. She was taken to the casualty ward of the local hospital, where her wounds were dressed and her fractured wrist was put in plaster.

'I suppose you're going to take me back to Holly Road,' said Molly miserably.

'I don't quite think so,' said the sergeant. 'We've something better in mind than that, starting with a hot meal. I don't suppose you've ever been in our police canteen.'

She shook her head. She had been in most of the rooms and cells in the police station, but never the police canteen.

By now the word had gone round that Molly was a hero, and policewoman Fulford took her gently in hand.

'Tell me all about it, Molly,' she said.

Molly did so.

'I don't think Holly Road is the best place for you, Molly,' she said. 'But I'll leave it to the local magistrates.'

Soon Molly found herself in the magistrates court, but not in the dock. She was sitting to one side in the public benches.

The magistrates were told what had happened, and the chairman of the bench, with a smile more benign than Molly had ever seen, commended her for her actions.

'Can we find somewhere nice for her until this matter is dealt with?' he asked.

The probation officer came forward at once with a suitable suggestion. This was the first time in her life that Molly had ever been made to feel welcome, and the police agreed to drop the existing charges against her.

But the old lady for whom she had risked her own safety, had plans of her own, which were acceptable to the authorities. She was a widow, and her husband had been the owner of the main bakery in town. She saw to it that Molly was given training – and a modest wage as well - for working in the baking industry. Molly proved a grateful and willing trainee, and developed a talent for it which surprised everybody, including herself. She married a likeable young food inspector, and that was the last of her criminal career.

As to Randy Griffin and Jogger Martin, they continued on the downward path until they found themselves in prison for 10 years for armed robbery. The Holly Road remand centre was put under a more progressive leadership, and is now a model of its kind.

THE UNEXPECTED VICTIM

Grant Wetherby folded his arms, and looked steadily at Mr. Armstrong, the cancer specialist.

'There's no doubt about it?' he said.

'None,' said Armstrong. 'You've seen the x-rays.'

'Up on your screen, yes. Does the white section show how far the cancer has reached in my liver?'

'In your liver, yes.'

'Couldn't you just cut that bit out?'

'Maybe. But what I can't cut out are the white filaments elsewhere which show how far the cancer has spread. You can see some of them here.'

'There might be more?'

'Certainly. Having reached this state, there's no telling quite how much further they may have spread. If the cancer has taken hold in your brain, or other important organs, I'm afraid that's it.'

'Inoperable?'

'I'm afraid so.'

'How long have I got then, Mr Armstrong?'

'There's no telling. It might be three months – even six months – probably not much longer. On a worst-case scenario, it could be only a few weeks.'

'Can I do anything to prevent it?'

'Prevent it, no. Postpone it by rest and quiet, yes. That is the best treatment for almost all medical conditions. If you start to get pain, we have means of dealing with that.'

'All right,' said Grant. 'I've already made my will, and my other affairs are in order. So, if death is inevitable, I may as well lie back and enjoy it.'

'That's the positive point of view I so like to hear from my patients. Keep in touch. I'm the always ready to do anything reasonable.'

Grant left the room, and made his way steadily out of the hospital. As he walked down the High Street, he noted all that the shops had to offer. AMAZING BARGAINS! said a notice in a clothes shop window. Everything at half price or less! This offer can't last forever.

'Nor can I,' thought Grant to himself with a chuckle. Then he came to a bookshop, with a cheerful-looking book in the window.

50 THINGS TO DO BEFORE YOU DIE! was its title.

‘I'd better have a look at this,‘ thought Grant. ‘Let's see what I could do in the time I've got left! If I knew anybody else with a condition like mine, we could have a sort of race to the cemetery, the winner making a donation to his favourite charity.‘

He started laughing so heartily that the girl in the bookshop was quite worried. He picked the book up quickly, and started to leaf through it.

See the Taj Mahal by Moonlight, was one entry.

‘That’d be no good; I wouldn't have time to get there.‘

‘Go to the top of the Eiffel Tower on a fine day, and admire everything. ‘I already did it many years ago,‘ he thought.

‘Go to the Serengeti game reserve, and see all the wild animals.‘

‘Been there and done that too,’ he thought. So it proved with many of the suggestions the book had to offer. Others he discounted because they simply didn't interest him. The book did not suggest going over the Niagara Falls in a barrel, but then it was doubtful if anybody could survive that experience. He noticed that the girl in the bookshop was staring at him, so he bought the book and put it in his pocket.

Back home, he read through all the different items and reached no other conclusions. I better think of something else for myself, he thought.

‘I know! I could commit a murder! Even if they caught me, they would be unlikely to visit me with any drastic punishment. On the other hand, I would spend my declining days in the prison hospital. Almost any hostel would provide more comfort, and more congenial companions and nurses.

Now, he thought, what sort of murder should I commit? I don't have any firearms. There must be sleazy pubs where pistols could be bought cheaply. But I don't want to visit them, and I doubt if I'm much good with a pistol. Besides, if I fired any shots, I should be bound to be caught. That would involve time in custody.

What about poison? I expect arsenic and strychnine are effective enough, and the same goes for potassium cyanide. I doubt if I could walk into a chemist's shop and buy them just for the asking. I think potassium cyanide is used for photographic purposes, but a few questions from the chemist would soon show I was no serious photographer.

What about brute force? That's no good. I was hopeless at boxing when I was at school, and I'm a good deal less agile and a good deal more podgy than then. That leaves a knife. I don't fancy a dagger sort of thing, because it brings me far too close to the victim, who could disarm me.

Grant thought for a while.

'I know!' He said to himself with some triumph, 'a sword-stick is what I'm looking for. I could walk the streets quite happily, and nobody would know I had that weapon. Then, if I chanced to find a situation where extreme violence was called for, I could put it to good use. I might even end up deemed a hero! That would add spice to my obituary!'

Grant was highly delighted with his plan, and wondered where he could buy a sword stick. A computer gave him a number of addresses and prices. For £60 he could get a very decent one. That only left one final problem. Who was he going to murder? Life was full of people who ought to be taught a lesson, but running them through with a sword stick was a bit much. Traffic wardens and income tax inspectors do perform a useful function, after all.

He looked through the daily paper. There were quite a number of good candidates for his sword-stick in Africa, but he was by no means certain he could get there before his strength gave out. But there were other notorious figures closer to home. There was Bill "Bigmouth" Brabbins, the leader of the All-comers's Union. He had a finger in many pies, and had started many a massive strike. The union conference was being held in Blackpool. He read that Brabbins regularly strolled along the promenade during the lunch break. It would be easy enough for him to stroll there as well, and apply the fatal thrust. The country would be well rid of Brabbins.

So he booked into the best hotel in Blackpool. A lot of members of Parliament stayed there, but not union reps, who tended to have lunch at a pub on the prom. So Grant set off at lunchtime with his sword stick, and walked the length of the promenade without seeing Brabbins. Possibly he had got delayed. He went to the main bar in the Coach and Horses, and asked if Big Bill was there.

'He's just gone out,' said the barman. 'Like as not, you'll catch him on his way back to the conference. You can't miss him!'

'Hopefully not,' said Grant, and hurried out. Sure enough, Big Bill was ahead of him. . Grant could have stabbed him from behind, but he wanted his victim to know his fate. He overtook Big Bill, then turned and drew his sword stick, the point resting on his heart.

'You've been shouting the odds long enough,' he said.

'Oh aye?' Said Big Bill, thrusting his hands calmly into his pockets. He had faced threats before.

'Yes,' said Grant. 'You've caused enough trouble in this country.'

'Sit down,' said Big Bill, pointing to a seat nearby, 'and put that thing away.' Grant sheathed his swordstick.

'You're an expert on politics, are you?' said Big Bill.

'I read the Daily Record,' said Grant.

'A rag,' said Big Bill, 'written by the ignorant for the ignorant. That's all you know of real life, isn't it. '

'I wouldn't say that,' said Grant. 'I was a personnel officer in a big concern which employed hundreds of workers, so I knew exactly who was stirring up trouble. You were at the back of it, usually.'

'No,' said Big Bill, 'I was always at the front of it. That's my mission in life, to fight for the workers with gloves off. There's been a long period with no wage rises. Did you know that?'

'I suppose so,' said Grant, 'but it's the same for everybody.'

'Including the bankers, I suppose.'

They've got to earn a good wage to keep the country going.'

'Including the bosses who retire with golden handshakes and bonuses when they leave, after a year of record losses. Being paid to go away before they do any more harm.'

'I wouldn't put it quite like that,' said Grant.

'Nor would I,' said Big Bill. 'It'd seem much worse if you were a working-class man, and saw your wages going down year after year while prices went up.'

'But statistics – '

‘Bugger statistics. Come and talk to Jack Prendergast. Here, Jack, this mate of mine, wants to learn the real facts of life. He reads the Daily Record.‘

Jack almost fell off his bar stool laughing.

Tell us,‘ said Big Bill, ‘what this last year has been for you.‘

Jack stared at the floor. ‘If you insist,‘ he said. ‘First of all, I lost my son to one of these roadside bombs in Afghanistan. . He was travelling in a vehicle clad in paper-thin armour when a roadside bomb did for him. Maybe he was lucky – a lot of his mates lost some of their limbs, and gained pennies in compensation. Then my missus went into a sink hospital with a serious complaint. She doesn't have any complaints now, I can assure you. So I'm living in an empty house with only my trade union activities to make life worth living.‘

‘I'm sorry,‘ said Grant. ‘I didn't know things were that bad.‘

‘Well, they are,‘ said Big Bill. ‘Run me through, for all I care.‘

‘And me too,‘ said Jack. ‘But make sure you've got a good alibi. Your party will need all the votes it can get at the next election.‘

That was Grant's first revelation. Back home, he thought things over. He was just planning to go to bed when he felt a fearful pain in his lower back. It was all he could do to drag himself up the stairs, and two days later he went back to see Mr. Armstrong.

A new set of x-rays was up on his screen, and he shook his head sadly. The cancer has reached your spine, he said. You may only have a few days now. I'll book you in at the Shakeshaft Hospice.

Grant found himself in a charming little hospital. The staff could not be kinder, and his pain levels were monitored every few hours. They had a lovely conservatory full of flowers, and there Grant saw a beaming smile.

It was Big Bill, who shook him warmly by the hand.

'Reached your spine, has it?' he said? 'Me too, I'm afraid. I wonder who'll be the first to go!'

'I didn't know you were in this condition,' said Grant.

'Nobody did,' said Big Bill. 'I'd have been written off as a has-been.'

'So you kept quiet about it.'

'Had to,' said Big Bill. 'Obstinacy in the face of facts. Some people might call it courage. But that's over now. We've a few days to see which of us is the better man. What's it to be, dominoes or darts?'

THE VANITY PUBLISHER

Bernie Shadwell went home with an armful of mail collected from his Post Office Box Number. One item in particular attracted his attention: a slim package addressed in old-fashioned handwriting and violet ink. A Mrs. Widgery of Barnstaple had sent him a collection of her poems, headed TRIXIE THE PIXIE.

The first one started

Trixie the Pixie is my pup,
He also is my chum.

Bernie read no more.

'Dear Mrs. Widgery,' he typed with two nicotine-stained fingers, using the palaver Wally Goggins had taught him, 'I am deeply grateful to you for sending me your poems. They touch a very special place in the heart, and would appeal to many readers.'

All she had to do was to send him a cheque for £1000 – 'printing costs are always high' – and she would receive five free copies of the book when published, together with 50% of the net profits.

'It would be as well to act quickly in this matter,' he added. The current demand for this kind of poetry may not last.'

Her cheque arrived by return of post.

A Mr. Keith Shovel sent him a hefty manuscript entitled 'FACTS ABOUT STOKE POGES.'

Bernie opened it at random near the end.

'The City Council controversy at p. 179', he typed, implying that he had read the whole book. 'over the Clonk Street gasometer, is particularly telling. The work should appeal to all those who hold Stoke Poges dear to their hearts.'

These letters he printed out on his 'Wise Minerva Press' stationary, quality paper headed with large gold lettering and the outline of an owl in royal blue. He signed the letters 'Bernard Shadwell, `Managing Editor.'

Wally Goggins put him up to this particular swindle.

'Vanity publishing is a good scam,' advised Wally. 'Lots of la-di-da authors will pay good money to see their codswallop in print.'

They shared a cell while Wally was doing three years for fraud. (Bernie had been convicted of persistent shop-lifting.) If there was one thing Wally knew about, it was style.

'First of all, you've got to change your vocabulary,' he said.

'Keep it short and simple?' asked Bernie.

'No, no,' said Wally severely. 'Use long words and phrases. 'Unobtrusive elegance,' for example. 'It suggests depth and style. Style's what counts, and first impressions. I'll teach you.'

Which he did.

Bernie became a very smooth operator indeed.

'I could call my outfit The Minerva Press,' mused Bernie, Minerva being the Goddess of Wisdom.'

'Nice one,' said Wally.

'But I think there may be another Minerva Press already,' said Bernie.

'All the better,' said Wally. 'You cash in on an established reputation. But go one better. Call it the 'Wise Minserva Press,' and back it up with fake testimonials to your product.

'In a class of its own.' – Express.

'Elegance personified' – Guardian.

'Astonishing value for money', - Telegraph.

'Which Telegraph?' asked Bernie.

'Please yourself,' said Wally. 'They probably won't bother coming after you, anyway. And use a Post Poffice Box-number address. Much more difficult for people to trace you.'

Bernie took his advice, and the money rolled in. So did the complaints, after a certain passage of time.

`I hoped I'd have received my five free copies by now,' wrote Mrs. Widgery.

'Market research has shown that your book would be even more successful if illustrated,' replied Bernie. 'That would cost a further £500.'

She sent him the cheque.

Keith Shovel was not so amenable. Nobody can produce a whole book of Facts about Stoke Poges without being exceptionally persistent.

`Unless I get a satisfactory reply within seven days,' he wrote, 'I shall place the matter in the hands of solicitors.'

'I am deeply pained to hear from you in those terms,' replied Bernie. 'The Wise Minerva Press prides itself upon good customer relations. It is only adverse trading conditions worldwide which have delayed the publication of your book.

May I ask you to bear with us a little longer?'

Nevertheless, he took advantage of the 7-day ultimatum to do a bunk, leaving behind him a pile of unpaid bills and unanswered letters. He moved to another city, acquired a different Post Office box number, and now operated under the title of 'The Ivanhoe Imprint.'

The manuscripts and cheques of optimistic authors continued to flood in.

It led to his downfall. Alison Grainger, of Peterborough, sent him a manuscript entitled 'Out of the Darkness.

Bernie read the first page.

'Some things in life,' it began, are too awful to think about. If you closed this book immediately, no-one could blame you.'

But Bernie read on. Alison went on to describe the first of many appalling incidents with her brutish father.

Bernie kept turning the pages, because he had to. It was so like his own story. He was removed from the custody of his parents at the age of seven, and not a minute too soon. He was already a problem child, and passed rapidly through the hands of several foster parents, who could not cope with his disturbed behaviour. Then he was transferred from institution to institution. Sometimes he escaped from them by running away. More often he escaped into the world of his own imagination, till he could hardly tell where reality ended. He created himself as an air ace, a fearless explorer, and the daredevil driver of a Formula One racing car.

Fantasy was his niche in life, and he went shoplifting only to obtain the things he felt the world owed him in any event. He had never been a great one for books. But Alison's book so gripped him that he had to publish it. He begged, borrowed or stole what he needed, and his friends from prison helped him. Jack Lightfoot, an expert forger of bank-notes, designed him a brilliant cover. Now he had copies of a book worth reading, and one landed on the desk of the Literary Editor of the Chronicle, who proclaimed its value immediately. Sales rocketed, and Bernie appeared with Alison on television.

For the first time in his life he had done something to be proud of. His values changed overnight, and he had enough money to publish other books. He became, in a small way, a celebrity, and Keith Shovel picked up his trail. Mrs. Widgery did nothing; she had died a year earlier, and her death certificate attributed it to 'natural causes.' She herself might have said it was from a broken heart.

The police traced many of his other victims as well. The judge sentenced him to two years' imprisonment, and ordered his funds to be distributed as compensation to his victims.

Prison yet again was no great hardship to Bernie. He knew he deserved it, and he took advantage of the opportunities which Lydenhall Open Prison offered him. He was put in charge of the prison library, and explored so many famous books that the time passed all too quickly.

He went to writing classes, and learned how to turn his experiences into vivid prose. As he did so, he saw clearly all the wrongs that had been done to him, and all the wrongs that he had done to other people. After setting them down on paper, he felt fresh and clean.

Mr. McFarlane, the `Prison Governor, gave him permission to send out his manuscript, entitled *The Tunnel.*

He contacted all the publishers he thought would be interested. Each day was an agony of suspense as he waited for a reply. Finally, after several weeks, one of item caught his eye immediately. 'I enjoyed reading it,' it said.

He sat down on his bunk, hardly daring to breathe. Then he pulled himself together, and read the whole letter.

'Dear Mr. Shadwell,', it began, 'thank you for sending me *The Tunnel.* But it is too similar in content and style to the existing book *Darkness* to justify our publishing it. I wish you every success in finding another publisher.'

He could think of no more publishers to write to. But George Fordyce, another prisoner, gave him the name of a new publisher he had heard of – the Architrave Press. Bernie sent off the manuscript immediately.

He was absolutely delighted when he got a reply only two weeks later, typed on high-quality paper, with 'The Architrave Press' printed at the top in elegant gold letters, with the design of a classical Greek portico outlined in royal blue.

'Dear Mr. Shadwell,' it began, and spoke in glowing terms of his book's quality. It had a special quality all of its own, would touch many people's hearts, and filled an important niche for the reading public. The letter continued over the page. All he had to do, to ensure publication, was to send them a cheque for

£1000, to defray the high cost of printing. He would receive no fewer than ten free copies of the book upon publication, together with a generous 60% of the net profits.

'Your prompt answer would be appreciated,' it concluded.

THE VITAL SPARK

Gregory Norcross was in high good humour as he strode along Dacre Street towards the splendid town house of Basil Hazeldean, the eminent Natural Philosopher. (Later they were called 'scientists.') He was learned, thorough, and widely read. His manner was unfailingly courteous. He was the ideal person to be the President of the Fortescue Society, named after their distinguished forebear, Sir Matthew Fortescue, the Astronomer Royal.

Sir Basil was due to retire. Gregory had no difficulty in guessing who the next president would be - himself, of course. Only Basil rivalled Gregory for experience and achievement. Basil had invited Gregory to call on him - presumably to congratulate him upon his forthcoming succession, and to offer a few useful suggestions about the running of the Society.

Gregory reached Basil's house. He was wearing a stylish dark blue coat with silver buttons, on which a Dolphin was carved.

The house was tall and dignified, like Basil himself. On this lovely autumn evening, the lamplighter was doing his rounds through the gas-lit streets of which Bellford was so justly proud. There was nothing old-fashioned about Bellford – gaslit streets were a proud modern advance of civilization.

Basil's house was gaslit too. Gregory rang the bell, and Flora the housemaid answered it.

'The Master is expecting you,' she said, and ushered Gregory into the library, where Basil was. A cheerful fire was burning there. And on a side-table was a tray with a fine decanter of sherry, and two glasses.

'I shall not be needing you further tonight,' Flora,' said Basil. It was her night off.

Thank you very much, sir,' she said, with a deferential bob of her knees, and left the room.

'I expect you can guess why I have asked you to come here tonight, Gregory,' said Hazeldean.

'Next week's meeting.'

'Most certainly. I shall be retiring then after ten years as President.'

'A most distinguished ten years.'

Hazekdean brushed the compliment aside with a wave of his hand.

'I nominated you to succeed me as President because of your own merit in the Natural Sciences. As you know, the qualities of electricity are of great interest to me. There is no saying how far they may go. Your paper on Positive and Negative Currents in electricity wsas regarded as very far-reaching.'

'Thank you,' said Gregory delighted.

'There are, of course, other pioneers in the field of electricity.'

'Indeed so. I move in distinguished company.'

'Such as Dr. Eschenbach of Leipzig University,' said Hazeldean, giving no hint of what was coming.

"I have corresponded with him on the subject,' said Gregory affably.

'So have I,' said Basil ominously.

Gregory stared at him.

'He has written a paper on the same subject as yourself.'

'Pioneers in the same field often reach the same conclusions at the same time,' said Gregory. "That is nothing new.'

'No, but his paper was published one year before yours, and you copied it word for word.'

'That is a monstrous thing to say!' said Gregory. It would make me guilty of plagiarism, as serious a crime as a scientist can commit. I would be utterly unworthy to become President of the Fortescue Society.'

'I entirely agree, said Basil. 'Here is a copy of his paper. Its date is one year before you gave your own paper.'

'What a coincidence!' said Gregory.

'But you wrote asking for a copy of his paper. Oh yes,' said Basil. 'He has written to me to say that he did.' He showed it to Gregory. 'May I have that letter back, please?'

'No!'; shouted Gregory, and hurled it into the fire. It was burnt to ashes. 'So what will you do now?'

'I have already prepared a letter to our Secretary. If you had been willing to resign discreetly from the Society, everything could have been hushed up. But you have lied to me and destroyed that letter. You leave me with no alternative. I am giving instructions that you should be struck off from the Society forthwith. I am sure that will happen.'

He took a letter from a drawer in his desk, and took a s stick of scarlet sealing wax from the desk, and warmed the end of it in a candle flame. Then he spread a blob of the hot wax onto the flap of the envelope, took off his signet ring, and pressed it onto the wax, thus sealing it.

'Can we not come to some arrangement?' said Gregory hoarsely.

'Certainly not,' said Basil.

'I could put the Society handsomely in funds – '

'Leave the house, said Basil, icily. 'You know your way out.'

Gregory left without another word, his head bowed down, and the front door closed behind him. Basil picked up the envelope, and left the house, intending to deliver the letter to the Society that very night. He did not see Gregory, who was hiding in the shadows.

'You shan't tell on me! You shan't!' said Gregory from between clenched teeth. He seized Basil by the shoulders, and forced him to the edge of the pavement. Basil grappled with him, trying to break his hold, but Gregory was too strong for him, and flung him into the path of a stagecoach.

Stagecoach divers were not always sober and alert. The stagecoach knocked Basil down, killing him instantly. He died of a fractured skull. The driver, who was jolted into awareness when the horses plunged and reared, never saw how it happened. He never saw Gregory snatch up the envelope that Basil had dropped, and make good his escape. It was regarded simply a as a tragic accident. Gregory was informed of the death, and came to the next meeting of the Society, wearing the same dark blue coat. He entered the meeting coolly. Mr. Davis, the Secretary, greeted him at the door.

'You've heard what has happened,' he said. 'But the business of the Society must continue. We must elect a new President, or the Society cannot function.'

'So soon? This evening?' asked Gregory.

'Indeed so, Mr. Norcross, said Davis. 'We did exactly the same when Professor Whitney died ten years ago.'

'So we did.'

'Could you say a few words tonight in tribute to our late Present?'

"I would count it an honour and a privilege.'

'Then we will start with your tribute and your election. May I first introduce you to our new member, Dr. Michael Torrington, the distinguished geologist?'

'I read your paper on the way that glaciers have shaped our world,' said Gregory. 'It was very interesting. Come and sit beside me.'

'That will be a pleasure,' said Torrington. 'May I say how much I like your coat? Not least with its silver buttons.'

'My London tailor made them specially for me. I am glad ou like them.'

'But you have lost one of the buttons off your cuff. Is it on the floor somewhere?

'Not that I can see,' said Gregory. 'But if it is lost, my tailor can supply another.'

Davis called the meeting to order.

'Due to special circumstances, we have a change of progamme tonight,' he said. 'It is a practical demonstration by Professor Tunberg of the powers of electricity upon members of the animal kingdom.'

'Ah,' said Gregory, keenly interested.

'It is a very striking demonstration,' said Torrington. 'I saw it given in London.'

Dr. Tunberg came forward, and bowed.

'First of all,' he said 'when electricity is applied to the leg of a frog, it causes a muscular reaction.'

Surely not,' said Oscar Wimple, a foppish young man who drank too much. He would never have been allowed to join the Society if his father not had not been a Past President.

'Indeed so,' said the Professor. 'Perhaps you would like to see for yourself at close range.'

Wimpole came forward, and others smiled. They could guess what might happen.

'Mr. Evershed will assist me tonight,' said the Professor. 'He is wearing rubber gloves and a rubber apron to insulate himself against any shocks. Let me warn those present against coming in contact with the subjects of these experiments.'

Evershed wheeled in a trolley bearing a large number of Leyden jars.

‘`You will be familiar, gentlemen, I know, with Leyden jars.’ said the Professor. Each one produces a modest quantity of electricity. It is, one might say, a small electric battery. But when they are all connected together, the shock can be very severe. Hence the need for caution. And here we have one dead frog.’

‘Are you sure it is dead?’ asked Wimpole.

‘Feel it for yourself.’

Wimpole picked it up and put it down again hastily .

‘Ugh,’ he said, ‘it’s all clammy. But dead, of course.’

‘We will only use a single Leyden jar at this stage,’ said the Professor, so the shock will only be a mild one. You are perfectly safe at this stage, Mr. Wimpole.’

Evershed took a polished copper rod connected with one Leyden jar, and applied it to the frog, which jumped several inches and landed on Wimple’s hand.

‘Oh my goodness,’ he said, and fainted clean away.

He was immediately attended by two doctors who were present at the meeting, and restored to his normal self

‘If you are all ready, gentlemen,’ said Davis, ‘Mr. Wimpole’s temporary indisposition merely served to remind us that the next part of the experiment requires the greatest care, because it involves a human body, and a much stronger current. It is only a few years since Mary Shelley wrote her famous book *Frankenstein*. That was, of course, fiction; lovers of learning have yet to see whether it can be done. Mr. Evershed, please.’

‘This is the body of an executed criminal, or of some pauper, I take it?, said Gregory.

'Oh no, Mr. President, it is the body of our former President, Mr. Hazeldean himself.'

'This is an outrage,' shouted Gregory. 'It is in the worst possible taste. If he was still alive, he would never have countenanced such a thing. He would have condemned it in the strongest possible terms.'

'No, sir,' Davis said. 'Quite the opposite. We all know how difficult it is to obtain bodies suitable for scientific experiments.'

'Why was I not told of this proposal before?;' said Gregory angrily.

'Because, Mr. President, his will was only read this morning. In it he insisted that, before his body was finally committed to the grave, it should be made available for any experiment the Society wished. It is an opportunity not to be missed. May I add that, for decency's sake, the body is wearing drawers. That will not affect any experiment.'

Gregory chafed and fumed. He was embarrassed, and worried in case something untowards occurred. Nevertheless, he trusted his own self-control to carry him through the evening.

'Very well,' said Gregory, "I agree, but with the utmost reluctance.'

'I am most grateful,' said Professor Tunberg. 'We must remember that Mr. Hazelhurst died from a fractured skull. Whether that will greatly limit our experiments, or render them valueless, I cannot say. Now, Mr. Evershed, we will take the leg first.'

Evershed took the galvanic rod, and touched the thigh of the corpse, whose leg was slightly bent at the knee.

There was a loud buzz from the instrument, and the leg shot out to its full extent, catching Evershed in the pit of the stomach, and forcing him off the platform.

There was a sensation among the spectators.

'It is as well that the electrical contact was broken, or the effect might have been more crucial. You will understand the importance of everybody remaining in their seats. I will now place the body in a sitting position, to text the thorax.'Wimpole applied the rod to the thorax. Again there was a loud buzz upon contact, but Evershed continued to hold the rod against the dead body, whose lungs extended and contracted, giving out a hoarse breathing.

'Are you all right?' said Torrington, who noticed Gregory's condition.

'Yes, thank you,' said Gregory. He knew he had to go through with it, and face the body. If he were to cut and run away, questions might be asked. He sat in his chair as rigid ad a suit of armour.

'Now the neck,' said the Professor.

Al the muscles of the face came into play, the mouth and eyes opening and closing. To Gregory, it seemed that the eyes were fixed solely upon him. He clenched his fists so tightly together that they ached.

"We have almost finished now, gentlemen, but for our final experiment we shall use the maximum amount of current,' said the Professor. Gregory relaxed a little.

'The arm, now, please.'

'The forearm, which was lying on the counter, shifted restlessly backwards and forwards, a little, and pointed straight at Gregory.

He could stand it no longer, and leapt to his feet.

'It's a lie, a damned lie! Don't point that arm at me!"

He leapt to his feet, ran to the body, and knocked the arm aside. There was a bright flash, and the force of the current threw Gregory back onto the floor. He lay back in his chair, breathing hard. He had his arms folded across him, and it was easy to see that one of the silver buttons was missing.

The dead man's other arm ended in a closed fist. That fist slowly opened, and from it rolled a small round objet. It was a button, a silver button, with the distinctive dolphin design upon it.

'You have taken your revenge,' said Gregory in a hoarse whisper. Those were his last words; the shock of the electric current and the shock of the dead man's accusation were too much for him. Dr. McCreevey, one of those present, examined the body.

'He is dead, gentlemen,' he said. 'The vital spark is extinguished.'

No useful purpose would have been served by making his discovery public knowledge. The minutes of the Fortescue Society merely record the tragic death by electric shock of the newly appointed President.

UNHAPPY MEDIUM

The three of them sat round a small table in the darkened room, holding hands. Verity Carteret's hands were as gentle and soft as good soap and handcream could make them. Henry Grant had the strong rough hands of a builder; his wife, Fiona, had thin and nervous hands which trembled all the time.

Verity leant forward.

'Dorothy's here,' she said. 'Your daughter's here now.'

Verity's sweet face radiated such kindness that nobody, surely, could have doubted her sincerity. Her whole appearance invited trust; her simple black dress, trimmed with a little lace at the cuffs and neck, a modest string of pearls, and a floral perfume so light as to be almost imperceptible.

'My dearest darling,' said Fiona, 'she knows we are here, does she not, Henry?'

He gave her hand a little squeeze. He was not a fanciful man, and could not fancy for one moment that he was being deceived.

'She is so pleased to know you have kept the garden just as she left it,' said Verity, 'the peonies are splendid!'

Henry and Fiona sighed with pleasure. They had taken such trouble to keep the little garden just as Dorothy used to do.

'She has one other message for you,' said Verity. 'She is so happy on the Other Side, and she knows that one day you will all be together again.'

'Does she say anything else?' asked Fiona.

'I am afraid she has gone now,' said Verity. 'The Dear Departed often say only a few words.'

So the séance came to an end.

'Isn't she a lovely woman,' sighed Fiona, when she had gone. 'So deeply caring. When we rang her to come here, weren't you impressed by the way she asked to see Dorothy's room, so that she could be alone with her vibrations, and find it easier to reach her on the Other Side? She would never have asked for a penny piece if she had failed.'

Nor would she. But she always succeeded. Verity used the opportunity to learn as much about Dorothy as she could. She quietly went through her belongings, and found the reference to peonies in her diary.

She could also assess how much the Grants could afford to pay. It would have been a great mistake to charge too little - people tend to think that what is cheap is not worth having. Instead, she charged them £75.00, which was quite a lot of money to them. She could tell that from the worn tablecloth and cheap cake when they sat together over a cup of tea.

But it meant they were making a sacrifice. They were so glad to do it, for Dorothy's sake.

'Shall we see you again?' they asked when the séance was over.

'I would not advise it,' said Verity. 'She sent you her love, and all too often a Dear Departed cannot say as much a second time. She might only disappoint you if she could not reach you. Besides, there are Alien Forces out there. Sometimes, I am their main target. I do not like to take unnecessary risks. I could be no help to you then. Sometimes their malevolence is aimed at people like yourselves. They might bring messages which are unforgivably evil, and would ruin your happiness.'

It showed them how sweet and caring Verity was.

Back home, Verity changed into a pair of plum-coloured slacks with a matching top.

'Sometimes I feel ashamed to take their money,' she said wistfully.

'You shouldn't, said Ralph, her husband. "You've fulfilled all their fondest hopes. They wanted to speak to their daughter again, and now they have done. So they believe.'

'Whatever made me get into this line of work?' she sighed.

'You remember perfectly well. It was when your mother was dying, years ago, and you went to see her every day in the hospital.'

'So it was,' said Verity. It meant a lot of time and effort on her part, but her mother was so glad of it.

'You're such a comfort to me, Verity,' she said. 'Always be a comfort to people. They need it so much.'

'I can't be a comfort to them, once they're dead,' said Verity.

'I expect you could,' said her mother, and closed her eyes.

Verity thought about it. She could be a comfort to friends and relatives, if they only knew that their loved one was happy, and that they'd be all together again some time.

'That's what they want to believe,' she said to herself, 'that's what they want to hear.'

Thus her career as a medium was born. The first time she ever held a séance, she was terrified that her clients would jump up and denounce her as a fraud. But it never happened; she uttered the words of comfort, and they could not thank her enough.

'Perhaps it's not so wicked after all,' she thought. 'After all, doctors prescribe placebos for patients which have no effect at all, save to cheer them up. She felt better after that.

On the very night that she was holding her séance with the Grants, and only five miles away at Hampton Green, Judy Keating, a pretty girl in her late teens, left the dance at the Village Hall.

'Want us to see you home?' asked her friends.

'No thanks,' said Judy briskly, 'I'm only two minutes walk away.'

She left on her own. It was a soft warm night, and the lilacs were in bloom.

A mustard-coloured van pulled up just ahead of her. The driver, Mark Chingford, a man in his fifties with a frank open face and smiling eyes, wound down his passenger window.

'Want a lift, young lady?' he said.

'No thanks,' said Judy. 'I'm nearly home now.'

‘But don’t you realise, young lady, at this time of night,’ he said urgently, ‘that (mutter mutter mutter)…’

He dropped his voice so that his last words could not be heard.

‘I’m sorry, I didn’t quite catch that,’ said Judy, bringing her face closer to the window.

That was the trap. He seized her by the neck, and dragged her in to the van. One cruel hand was round her mouth, so that she could hardly make a sound.

’Somebody help me, please. PLEASE!’ she whispered.

His other hand forced a thick pad steeped with chloroform over her nose.

That was the last thing she ever knew, mercifully.

Unspeakable things were done to her body, alive and dead, followed by expert work with sharp knives.

The following morning, Pamela, Judy’s mother, reported her daughter missing. The police learnt at once from a closed-circuit video of the High Street, which van it was, and who was driving it. They arrested Mark Chingford immediately.

His explanation was simple and unshakeable.

‘I know I dragged her into the van,’ he said, ‘but she cried so much that I took pity on her, and let her go a mile further down.

The police examined the van minutely and noticed the smell of chloroform, but they could prove nothing further. They never found the body, though they searched every single place where they thought Mark might have hidden it.

Under those circumstances, he was convicted of kidnapping (snatching her into his van was in itself kidnapping), and was sentenced to five years imprisonment. But he refused to admit that he had killed her or to say where the body now lay.

Pamela, her mother, was distraught. She employed a private investigator for a full month to check what Mark's movements were, and where he came and went. It proved nothing.

Then she rang up Verity Carteret.

'You're my last hope,' she sobbed, 'Judy was all I had to live for.'

'I quite understand,' said Verity.

'But you can't know it all,' said Pamela. 'My husband walked out on me five years ago, for another woman. He read about Judy's disappearance on the news, and all he could say was 'That's tough. I expect she'll turn up some day. Perhaps she wanted to walk out too.' That was cruel of him, wasn't it?'

'Desperately cruel,' said Verity. 'He couldn't have had anything to do with her death, could he?'

;'The police thought of that, but he had a cast-iron alibi. He was in Majorca with his fancy woman. And, of course, the police had the video which showed her being kidnapped.'

'Then you'd like a séance, at your house? To see if I can get in touch with Judy? '

'Yes, please,' said Pamela. 'If it isn't asking too much,' she added miserably. She had had so many disappointments.

So Verity went, and, as usual, was shown Judy's photographs, and asked to see her room.

Pamela picked up a charming toy rabbit. It had pink nylon fur, a sweet smile, and stiff whiskers.

This is Fluffy, her favourite toy,' she said, and handed it to her. But the moment Verity touched it, icy fingers seized her wrist in a steely grasp, and would not let go. She could actually see Judy's face, showing up deathly pale, against the dark wood of a cupboard. Her eyes were wide with terror.

She could smell the acrid and overpowering stench of chloroform.

Verity sank down onto a chair. Her breath came and went rapidly, her face as pale as Judy's.

'You've seen her, haven't you,' said Pamela.

'Yes,' said Verity, 'I truly have, She said, Please, please help me.'

'Somebody help me, please. PLEASE!' Judy gasped desperately.

'She must be dead, otherwise you could not have seen her,' said Pamela.

'That must be so.'

'If you held a séance immediately, she might tell us where she is, and how she died.'

'I suppose so,' said Verity quietly, never having spoken to a dead person before.

She was desperately afraid of what might happen. She could not take refuge in phrases like 'She is very happy on the Other Side.' All she could see, when the room was darkened, was Judy's face, her eyes nearly out of their sockets in terror.

She could small the acrid and overpowering stench of chloroform.

'You are here, aren't you, Judy?' she asked.

'Ahhhhhhh,' was the only response, a long drawn out sob.

'Your mother is here, Judy,' she said. 'Can you tell us what happened to you?'

'Somebody help me,' moaned Judy.

'Can you tell us where you are? Where your body now lies?'

'Please help me. PLEASE!' said Judy.

'Your mother needs to know so desperately.'

But there was silence, and Judy's face faded away into nothing.

'It's no good,' Verity confessed when the séance was over, 'I made no progress'.

'You reached her, at least,' said Pamela. 'We can always try again.'

So they did, three times a week. Verity never asked for payment; she felt she was expiating all her years of fraud and deceit.

There the matter rests. At every séance, and in the stillness of the night, Verity feels the icy fingers round her wrist, and sees Judy's face with the despairing eyes. She hears the words 'Please help me,' and the stench of chloroform is strong in her nostrils.

It cannot last forever. Verity is ageing rapidly, her cheeks hollow and careworn, and her hair whiter and thinner. She wears heavy perfumes now, to try and mask the smell of chloroform, and her wrist has grown rheumatic from the pressure of icy fingers. Perhaps, one day, Judy's body will be found, and there will be a release from the present state of things.

Perhaps not.

YES WE HAVE NO PIRANHAS

Eddie Podmore looked at his watch.

'The taxi should be here in five minutes,' he said.

There was a ring at the door.

'Good,' he said, 'punctuality is what I always like to see.'

You're not always punctual, Gladys thought. But she did not like openly to correct the head of the family.

He opened the door, and Gladys stepped forward with her suitcase. Their two children did the same. But it was not the taxi; it was a man in a green and white uniform with a peaked cap, on which was the word Waterfords.

'Special Delivery,' he said. 'Sign here, please.'

He put a package down on the floor, and handed Eddie a form to sign, which he did.

'That's it, then, mate,' he said cheerfully, and returned to his van.

'Who's it for?' Said Gladys. 'We weren't expecting anything.'

The package said LIVESTOCK. THIS SIDE UP. DO NOT REFRIGERATE.

'We didn't order any livestock,' said Gladys.

She turned accusingly towards the children. 'You haven't gone and ordered any livestock, have you?'

'No,' said Tommy. He was a very positive young man of nine. 'What about you, Monkey?' He said, turning towards his sister.

Her real name was Monica, but Tommy had called her Monkey for years.

'No, I didn't,' she said.

'You must have,' said Tommy. 'None of us did, so it must be you.'

'It wasn't,' said Monica, getting cross.

Eddie intervened. 'You've just started biology. Are you sure you didn't order any frogs or tadpoles, something like that?'

'No, I didn't, I didn't,' said Monica, bursting into tears.

'Let's just see what it says on the label,' said Gladys calmly, whilst giving her a big hug to soothe away her tears.

'It's addressed to Mrs. Rossiter, 47 Clevely Crescent,' said Eddie.

'There's never been a Mrs. Rossiter here within living memory,' said Gladys. 'Unless – '

She looked suspiciously at Eddie. It wasn't that she didn't basically trust him, but you know what men are.

'You remember that week last April when I went down to see my parents,' she said. 'You didn't have any ladies in then, did you, Alfred Podmore?'

'Certainly not.'

'I found all the flower pots had been moved round when I came back,' she said, 'so I wondered what was going on.'

'I was trying out a new garden fertiliser. The lads at the pub recommended it to me. To make the flowers develop faster.'

'They did indeed,' said Gladys. 'They died in a week.'

'It wasn't my fault,' said Eddie. 'It just seemed a good idea.'

'None of your Good Ideas are good ideas,' said Gladys. 'It was tomato fertilizer, anyway.'

'Hadn't we better open the package?' said Tommy.

So they did. The flap at the top of the stout cardboard carton was fixed with staples Eddie fetched a screwdriver and prised them away. He could see there was a plastic bag inside, but before he could take it out there was a ring at the door. It was the taxi.

'What are we going to do?' asked Eddie.

'We'll have to take it with us. We can't just leave livestock here to die,' said Gladys. 'We'll think of something.'

They got into the taxi. Five minutes later they were stopped at the traffic lights when Tommy shouted 'Look, Mum! There's the Delivery Van.'

It was facing them on the other side of the lights, having made another delivery. Eddie jumped out of the taxi.

'Don't leave without me,' he said, and ran round the front of the van. He tapped on the driver's window.

'Yes, mate?' Said the driver, lowering it.

'You delivered a package to 47 Clevely Crescent ten minutes ago.'

'That's right,' said the driver.

'It's for a Mrs. Rossiter. She doesn't live at 47 Clevely Crescent.'

'That's her problem', said the driver.

'You don't understand,' said Eddie. 'She doesn't live there. But it's her package, not ours, and we don't need it. You'd better take it back.'

'Can't, mate, you signed for it,' said the driver.

'But it's livestock. What am I supposed to do with it?'

The driver could have made a vulgar suggestion, but Eddie was well-built and angry. He thought better of it.

'Enjoy them, he said, and drove away. The lights had changed.'

The taxi arrived at the station. The train for Winkle Bay was not yet in. So they had time to examine the package at leisure.

'It's livestock, but very small livestock,' said Tommy. 'Perhaps it's Jersey cows.'

'It's too small to be Jerseys,' said Gladys.

'My Jersey was big enough to wear until you shrank it, 'said Eddie.'

'I put it in the washing machine on the wrong programme,' said Gladys. 'It was the only time in 15 years. Don't go blaming me.'

'Perhaps it's not cows, but mice,' said Tommy.

Monica gave a little shriek. 'I'm terrified of mice, ' she said.

'So are elephants,' said Tommy. 'Time you lost some weight.'

'You beast!' Said Monica.

'Double beast yourself,' said Tommy.

'You both belong in a zoo,' said Gladys. 'Let's open the package and get it over.'

It had a strong plastic bag inside, with two little fishes swimming about in it, rather drab in colour.

'They can't be goldfish,' said Eddie.

'Might be', said Tommy, 'after deflation.'

He was sometimes so witty you could scream.

Eddie read the label on the bag.

'It says Tropical Fish. Piranhas. Keep at a warm temperature 70-80 degrees Celsius.'

'They're South African, then,' said Eddie.

'South American,' said Monica, crossly. 'They come from the Amazon.'

'Amazon UK, more like,' said Tommy. 'You can get them on the Internet.'

'They're said to be very ferocious,' said Eddie, and put his finger cautiously into the top of the bag. He got a nasty nip.

'Ow!' He said, sucking his finger. It was bleeding profusely at the tip.

'Serves you right,' said Gladys. 'Trust a man to do something stupid.'

But Eddie had gone very pale.

'What do you get from being bitten by a fish?' He said.

'Blood,' said Monica, in a matter-of-fact way.

'I mean,' said Eddie, 'do you get anything else from being bitten by a fish? Rabies?'

'If it's a mad dogfish,' said Tommy.

'Piscine rabies is unknown to medical science,' said Gladys. She was a doctor's receptionist, so she knew. 'Hold still while I put a piece of sticking-plaster on that finger. We don't want you bleeding all over the place.'

She produced some from her capacious bag. She was always ready for emergencies.

'I know what I'll do,' said Eddie with determination. 'I'll flush these little blighters down the toilet.'

'You mustn't,' said Tommy in alarm. 'There are horror films about that. Somebody tips a baby alligator down the drain, and before you can say Jack the Ripper the New York sewers are full of alligators, breeding like rabbits.'

'They can't,' said Monica coldly. 'They're reptiles. Rabbits don't lay eggs.'

Eddie caught the eye of two passing policemen.

'Excuse me,' he said, 'do you deal with Missing Persons?'

'Certainly, sir,' said the officer. 'Have you lost any?'

'No,' said Eddie, 'I've found some fish.' He held up the bag. 'One of them bit me'.

The officer's eyes narrowed. 'Using your finger for bait, were you, sir?'

The second officer came closer. If Eddie was a dangerous lunatic, the sooner he was restrained, the better.

'Where do these fish come from, sir?' He asked.

'The Amazon.' Said Eddie.

'And I'm the Archbishop of Canterbury. If we have any more nonsense from you, sir, you'll be done for wasting police time.'

The officers strode away.

This is a fine start to our holiday,' said Eddie. They moved to the ticket barrier. Their train was already at the station platform.

'What have you got there, sir?' Asked the ticket inspector. 'I can see the word LIVESTOCK on the box.'

'It isn't actually livestock, it's fish,' said Eddie.

'Dangerous fish,' said Tommy with relish. He loved to cause a sensation.

'Dangerous fish,' said the ticket inspector thoughtfully. He consulted a manual. 'Have you got a ticket for them?'

'I know you need a ticket for a dog. I didn't know you needed one for a fish.'

'You might if it was a dog-fish, sir,' he suggested. 'But not if they were catfish.'

'They're not catfish.'

'Hm,' said the ticket inspector. 'Under railway regulations, things are dangerous if they're flammable or explosive. Are the fish inflammable?'

'No,' said Gladys firmly.

'Can they explode?'

'They might if they were balloon fish and you pricked them,' said Tommy.

'They're not balloon fish, they're piranhas,' said Eddie.

'All right, sir. I'll let you on the train if you will sign this form that the liability is entirely upon yourself if anything untoward happens.'

'Fair enough,' said Eddie, and he signed it, though his bitten finger made it awkward to hold the pen.

'Good,' said Gladys, 'now we can be on our way.'

'Not yet, madam,' said the inspector. 'Your train has gone, the next one is not for a couple of houses. But, in view of the circumstances, I have four £5 vouchers for you to use in the station buffet, where you can purchase the usual range of beverages and comestibles.'

They thanked him, banqueted upon Cola Cola and sandwiches, and put two plastic containers full of hot tea next to the bag with the piranhas, to keep them warm.

When they arrived at Winkle Bay, it was late afternoon. They left their luggage at their hotel, and went straight to the

Aquarium which Gladys remembered from a previous visit. On the way a thought struck her.

'In the Bible.' She thought, 'Jesus had the miracle of the five loaves and the two small fishes. We've had our own miracle.'

'May we present you with some fish: she said. 'They're piranhas.'

'That's interesting,' said the Curator. 'Let's have a look at them.'

They were carefully decanted into their own tank, but it was too late; they floated belly upwards on the surface of the water. The journey had been too much for them.

'You mustn't blame yourselves for this,' said the Curator. 'Thank you for your time and trouble. You did your very best. I will give you a free pass for the Aquarium during your stay here.'

They made use of it, and thoroughly enjoyed it. They returned home with healthy tans, refreshed in mind and body.

'Well,' said Eddie, as they entered the house and shut the front door, "that was everything our holiday should have been.'

They all agreed.There was a ring at the door. Mrs. Rossiter, as it proved to be, stood there looking like a championship boxer about to enter the ring.

'What have you done with my piranhas?' She demanded.